Thanks to my proofing team:

Bobby Politte

J. Fitzpatrick Mauldin

Mike Morrey

You guys are the best!

Published by Pandahead Publishing, a division of Pandahead Productions. Pandahead Publishing and the pandahead logo are trademark of Pandahead Productions.

Book and cover design by Pandahead Productions

Cover illustration by Valentina Barmina

Please visit www.publishing.pandahead.com

The publisher is not responsible for websites (or their content) that are not owned by the publisher.

The characters and situations in this book are fictitious. Any similarity to real persons, living or dead, is coincidental and not intended by the author.

Print ISBN: 978-1-944209-02-5

Ebook ISBN: 978-1-944209-03-2

DEDICATION

A special shout-out to Bobby Politte, who showed me an article about unusual, forgotten comic book characters which led me down this remarkable rabbit hole.

I would like to dedicate this novel to Len Short and all the other creators who have taken the time to craft something from their heart and imagination and share it with the world. It takes courage to do so, and even if someone says that they have been, they are not forgotten.

And a deepfelt dedication to my incredible wife, Allyson. Your love and support keeps me going.

-Brett Brooks

a Pussy
Katnip

novel

Red

is the

DARKEST
COLOR

Foreword - Who is Pussy Katnip?

Very little is known of the origin of the character of Pussy Katnip. She first appeared in *Green Mask #3* in 1940 and in a total of twenty-two stories spanning over twelve different titles from Fox Comics throughout the 1940's. The only creator name associate with the series was Len Short, but nothing is known of Mr. Short beyond his connection to Pussy Katnip—and even then, his name only appears in two stories.

The character was the result of the growing popularity of super-heroes and the steady popularity of anthropomorphic characters. Characters from Disney, Warner Bros, and many others were on movie screens across the country, side-by-side with the superhero serials of the day. So, add on the popularity of noir detective stories and you've got the perfect mix, right?

Well, maybe not.

Pussy never caught on. She and her cast of characters—many of which appear in this novel—faded away into obscurity, and ultimately, public domain.

Which is what put this novel in your hands. I was intrigued by the character from the moment I first heard about her from my friend (and co-creator of the popular *Sentinels* superhero novels from White Rocket Books) Bobby Politte. We were talking about one of our favorite subjects—comics—and he mentioned an article about bizarre characters, and ultimately, Pussy Katnip.

So, I read about her. And then I read her stories. All of them. They are all out there, as she is in public domain, you just have to work some internet-fu. And right off the bat, I knew I was going to be writing a story with her, which turned into the novel you hold now.

Of course, what you are about to read isn't really a "pure" version of the character. The first thing that I changed was her appearance. Though described as very beautiful in the comic, the actual design of the character defied that image rather strongly. I also tweaked her seemingly ever-changing powers as they appeared in the comics. I also streamlined her role at the Kit Kat Klub, making her the sole owner and star, which was sometimes nebulous in the comics. Plus, beyond the two-panel retelling of her having the formula for Katnip Fizz passed down from generation to generation, there wasn't much of an origin in the comics, so I developed it quite a bit.

Something you might notice when you read this is the fact that there are no guns in the story. Yes, it's a staple of pulp-noir, but they never showed up in any Pussy Katnip story, so they felt out of place here. There's plenty of action, but no guns. Just wanted to make sure you knew it wasn't an oversight.

I'm proud to bring you the first in what I hope is many novels featuring Pussy Katnip and her odd little world. It was fun to write, and I hope it is equally fun to read. There's only one thing left to say…

Welcome to The Kit Kat Klub.

> - *Brett Brooks*

Chapter One

The moment that his hand slipped free from the handle of the door, he was already reaching for it again. His left hand wiped across the front of his pants, as if drying it made a difference with the handle in his right.

Moving past the doorway, the warm air of the club welcomed him like an old friend as he stepped inside. The dim sound of music playing and the aroma of smoke and food pulled at him.

"Good evening, sir! Welcome to the Kit Kat Klub!" The friendly voice was even more accommodating. The counter almost hid the woman behind it, but she stood proudly, head high and shoulders back, a shock of red just peeking from under her pillbox hat.

"Uh, hi," he answered softly.

"Cold night, huh? Well, it's always warm in here," she chirped. "Would you care to check your coat tonight, sir?"

"Huh?" His eyes ventured down as though just discovering that he was, in fact, wearing such a garment. "Yeah, I guess."

Her eyes lingered on him for a moment, and then she leaned forward slightly. "First time here?"

His head shook back at her. "No. No, I just...." He swallowed. "That obvious?"

"Don't worry about it! You're among friends. I'm Robin." She extended her hand across the counter. He took it in his and shook it once. "Everything's fine. Give me your coat, and I'll slip you a ticket. When you're done, just come back out and pick it up. It's on the house."

The tip jar on the right side of the counter was just visible in his peripheral vision.

"Okay, thanks." He slipped the coat off and laid it on the counter, revealing an ill-fitting blue suit beneath. "Is...is Miss Katnip here tonight?"

"Always," she answered with a laugh. "Miss Katnip is the star of the house."

"Oh, good. Is she...?" His thumb gestured down the hall.

"Yeah. Just go on in and head to the bar. Robby's working tonight. He'll set you up with something to wet your whistle, and settle your nerves. Miss Katnip should be up in just a few, actually," Robin explained.

He nodded and looked down the hall, then back to the coat-check girl. With a wink she waved him on his way.

Only a few steps later the sounds of the band took over, forcibly easing each step as he moved to the top of the short set of stairs leading into the heart of the club. His hand locked on the rail and his feet shuffled as he took in the sight.

A half-dozen waitresses scampered across the floor, deftly moving between the tables and patrons with practiced precision, while still managing to balance a tray in one hand. The pressed white shirt and black pencil skirts must have matched Robin's outfit, based on the pillbox hat each of them wore.

Beyond the tables was a dance floor with a handful of couples milling about while the small band played. The band sat beside the small raised stage, with four men in white suits on drums, trumpet, upright bass, and piano, making music that sounded like it came from four times as many instruments.

Finally, he locked on the long bar running the left-hand side of the club. Relaxing his grip, he let go of the railing and stepped down to the floor, then walked to a seat that left at least one open space on either side of him. Without realizing it, his head turned again towards the stage, seeing only a lone microphone in the middle of it, with closed royal blue curtains hanging behind.

"What's buzzin', cousin?" His head jerked back around to find a thin man with black hair looking his way.

"I...well, that is, I came to see Miss Katnip," the man answered.

"You and every other mug in here, bud," the bartender stated. "What can I get you to drink in the meantime?"

"Uh, well, um...scotch, I guess." He reached into his jacket pocket and pulled out his wallet, then slipped a couple of bills from it and put them on the bar. "And I didn't mean that I was here to see Miss Katnip perform. Not entirely. I hear she's wonderful, but...oh, never mind. Just the scotch I guess."

The bartender's hand slipped out of site and returned with a glass and a bottle, though his eyes never left the man across from him, who was staring at the wooden surface between them.

"Neat or the rocks?"

"What?" The man looked up. "Oh, um, on the rocks, I guess. Please."

The glass disappeared once more, and a clinking sound of ice soon followed. "What's your name, pal? I'm Robby."

"Oh, I'm Todd." His hand came up near his body, with a finger directed back towards the entrance. "The nice girl at the front—Robin, I think—mentioned you."

"Did she now?" The corner of Robby's mouth turned up. "Yeah, well, she's a sweet cookie." He placed the glass in front of Todd and turned a bottle up over it, in just a couple of seconds two slugs of scotch poured out of the jigger, which he cut off with a slight bump and twist of the wrist. "So, what's your story? You seem like a man with something to say."

"Me? Oh, I...." His chest fell. "Nothing. I don't have a story." He reached out and wrapped his hand around the glass, feeling the damp condensation add to the moisture already in his palm.

"C'mon, don't be a pill, buddy! You said you was here to see Miss Katnip." Robby's head motioned to the stage. "She'll be up in a just a couple."

With more than a slight jag to his turn, Todd looked back at the stage, and then back to the bartender. "Does...well, that is to say, do you know if Miss Katnip ever sees any of the people who come to see her?"

Robby snorted softly. "Depends on who it is and what they want. You a fan?"

"I...truthfully, I've never heard Miss Katnip sing before." He picked up the scotch and took a small sip. "I was hoping that I might...." There was a moments pause, followed by Todd taking a much larger sip and then looking Robby in the eye.

"I've heard that Miss Katnip can help people. Sometimes at least. I was truly hoping that she might see me tonight."

"Oh." Robby nodded. "Well, y'see, Miss Katnip tries to keep a low profile, y'know? She's not the type who goes out and gets in trouble herself." Casually, Robby scratched under his chin. "But, just for conversation purposes, what is it you was wanting to talk to Miss Katnip about? You got law troubles?"

"What? No. No, nothing like that." Todd sat up straight. "The police and I…they haven't been an issue. In fact, they haven't been willing to talk to me much at all."

"Is that so?" Robby asked. "Well, the cops don't like folks from Mutt Town comin' to them too much. We ain't so high up on their important list."

The sound of the band coming to new life cut off not only their conversation, but everyone in the place, as all eyes turned to the spotlight that hit the stage. Several bars of music sounded through the room, slowly softening to a more manageable level. A palpable tension grew, like a child waiting on ice cream to be handed down, finally resolved when a woman stepped into the spotlight to enough applause to drown out the band. A male voice came from nowhere, "Ladies and gentlemen, The Kit Kat Klub proudly presents, Miss Pussy Katnip!"

She stood, waiting at the microphone, wearing a yellow striped dress someone seemingly poured her into. The long blond hair that fell down her back almost matched the tone of her dress, and offset the cream color of her face. A single strand of black pearls dangled around her neck, each one large enough to be a marble in some kid's game. Slowly, her hand came up to the mic and pulled it towards her.

And then her voice filled the room, deep and rich, like heaven come to Earth.

5

Brett Brooks

I've got a feeling in my mind,
About a man I've yet to find.
Every day it's him I see,
I just wish he'd look at me.

I've got you inside my dream.
I swear to you, it's not a scheme.
Every night I fade away,
Looking for someone to play,
Then I see you and start to say,
Hope you'll find me during the day.

People say I look tired,
But it's just my new attire.
I just want to wait for him,
In a dress that's very prim.

I've got you inside my dream.
I swear to you, it's not a scheme.
Every night I fade away,
Looking for someone to play,
Then I see you and start to say,
Hope you'll find me during the day.

Then's the part I'm so proud of,
That you walk into my love,
When you feel my loving heart,
My new life will finally start.

I've got you inside my dream.
I swear to you, it's not a scheme.
Still you aren't here now with me,
So I sing my heartfelt plea,
Don't you think it's time you came,
To the arms of this lonely dame?
What a shame…

'Cause I've got you inside my dream!

The applause from her appearance on stage was barely a whisper compared to the ovation following her song, and Todd was a welcome participant. He stood from his stool, eyes fixated on the captivating creature, which kept him from seeing Robby motioning towards Pussy.

Once again, the woman stepped to the microphone.

"Thank you." She paused for a moment. "It's nice to see so many of you folks coming out in this cold. I hope you're finding it a bit warmer inside the club."

The responding laughter was intercut with a smattering of applause—and a wolf whistle or two.

"It's also nice to see so many boys out here without their wives or girlfriends, too," she teased. "Of course you do realize that means your wives and girlfriends are on their own tonight too, right?"

The only thing breaking the laughter this time was the few silent areas of men considering her words.

"Well, the important thing is that you're here tonight, and we're going to do everything we can to make sure that you have a good time. Right now I'm proud to bring to the stage one of the newest talents here at the Kit Kat Klub. She's a sensational young singer that I'm sure you'll love, Miss Jenny Foal!"

The dark-skinned woman stepped through the curtains and onto the stage to a warm welcome, but it paled compared to the one Pussy received. Miss Jenny belted into a song as bright and strong as she could, still staying in the shadow of the woman who went before her.

Todd watched Pussy slip from the stage and made her way around the edge of the room. Every few steps someone stopped her, for this and for that, but each time she made her excuses and continued on her way. Watching her work her way closer, with each step he ran the words he wanted to say through his mind.

"She's really somthin', ain't she?" Robby's voice called him back, and he turned to face the bartender.

"Yes, she's…she's better than everyone said she was, actually," Todd answered.

"Well, it's kinda hard to put Miss Katnip into words. A song, maybe…." Robby laughed. "So, you still wantin' to talk to her?"

Todd nodded. "Yes. Very much so, but…well, so does everyone else, it seems. I doubt I even get close enough to say hello."

"Oh, I wouldn't say that."

The sultry voice behind him shocked Todd stiff. He turned slowly and saw a vision of beauty dressed in yellow not five feet away.

"Now's the time when you would say hello, actually," she chuckled.

"Hello," he replied mechanically.

"Hello to you." She pointed to the barstool beside him. "Is this seat taken?"

He looked over at it and blinked. "N-no. No, it's free."

"Good." She slipped onto the stool without a hitch in her step, then raised a single finger towards Robby, who responded with a short nod.

Todd turned back to his drink and downed the remainder is a single gulp. When he turned back, the lady beside him was looking his way.

"I'm Pussy Katnip," she extended her hand.

His lips got slightly ahead of his words, but they eventually found their way out as he shook her hand. "I...I'm Todd. Todd Crocker."

"It's a pleasure to meet you, Mr. Crocker." She pulled her hand back just as the bartender sat down a half-filled glass of clear liquid. "Thank you, Robert."

"No, Miss Katnip, it's my pleasure," Todd gulped.

"Please, call me Pussy." She took a sip and set the glass back down on the bar. "Now, Mr. Crocker, what is it that brings you in tonight? Just out for a night on the town?"

"I wish that were so, ma'am," he answered. "No. No, I'm in a bad state right now. I don't know where to turn."

"Sorry to hear that, Mr. Crocker, but what makes you think that I can help you?" Her whole body leaned in towards the bar, almost molding itself to the counter.

"I don't...." He shook his head. "I've heard people talk. They say things about you. That you...that you help others out, and, well, I was hoping...."

Her hand came out and rested gently on his. "Hoping for what, Mr. Crocker? What's wrong?"

His eyes lingered on her hand, but eventually made it up to look her in the face. "I made a mistake. My daughter—Abby, she's six—she got real sick. She's got asthma bad. I took her to the doc, but he said that she was gonna need to spend some time in the hospital, and the insurance folks were giving me a hard time, but I had to do something. I don't have that kinda cash. I'm just a regular guy. I work down at the water plant. So I took her to the hospital, and she was getting better, but...but

9

I went through my savings and my wife and I got desperate, so...."

He stopped, his voice breaking to the point where all the words that were pouring out of him simply couldn't go any further.

Pussy's voice spread over him like butter. "Do you need money, Mr. Crocker? Is that it? I can put in a good word for you down at the bank, and they—"

"No," he interrupted. "That's just it, I got the money. I paid the hospital, but now...now it's coming back to haunt me. I don't care that they threatened me, but not my wife and kid. I couldn't live with myself if something happened to them."

"Okay," Pussy pulled back her hand, "you're going to have to give me some more details, Mr. Crocker. What happened?"

"Like I said, I needed cash, and a guy I knew said that I could get it from Boss Dogg." His words made Pussy stiffen. "When I went to see him, he seemed nice, y'know? He sounded real worried about Abby and wanted to help. He got me the money right on the spot."

"And you're having trouble paying him back?" The butter of her words were laced with barbs.

"No, that's just it, I paid him back, with interest, even. And before it was due." Todd swallowed. "Just, now he says that things have changed. That I owe more. I don't have any more, Miss Katnip. I can't pay him anything else, and he sent his goons down to the plant and they said they were gonna show up at my house and...."

The sound of the song in the background was enough to hide the sobbing sound that followed. Pussy glanced over at Robby, and with a shift of her eyes said everything he needed to know. The empty glass in front of Todd started refilling. The moment that Robby pulled the bottle away, Pussy took hold of the glass and presented it to Todd.

"Here." He took it from her hand. "Now, I want you spend some time here and enjoy the evening, Mr. Crocker." Her voice was now butter with honey. "And when you go home, you need to hug your little girl and kiss your wife, and then get yourself a full night's sleep."

"What?" He blinked. "Are…are you going to help me? What are you going to do?"

"Mr. Crocker," Pussy stood from her bar stool and leaned in to kiss the troubled man on the cheek, "don't ask questions. Just go home. Everything is going to be just fine." She glanced over to Robby, who gave her a nod in return. "Goodnight, Mr. Crocker. It was a pleasure meeting you."

He watched her walk away, only realizing once she was gone that he hadn't said goodbye to her.

"I didn't get a chance to thank her," he mumbled. "I didn't even say goodnight."

"Hey, Buddy, don't worry," Robby's words turned him around, "Miss Katnip knows. She's got you covered."

"But, what's she going to do? She didn't tell me," Todd stated.

"Well, in just a few minutes she's gonna get on stage and sing another song, and that's all you need to worry about," he explained, "'cause you got a night here on the house."

"I just don't know what to say," Todd whispered.

Despite the volume, Robby seemed to hear him just fine. "Ya aint gotta say nothin', Buddy." He reached across the bar and slapped him on the shoulder. "In fact, don't. Nothin' happened here tonight, capisce?"

Todd nodded, as the music swelled to fill the club once more.

Red is the Darkest Color

Brett Brooks

Chapter Two

"Hey Boss!" He loped into the room, a cigarette dangling from his lips. The walls of the room were lined with dark-stained wood, providing a feeling of luxury, which was quickly dispelled by the lack of any flooring over the concrete slab underfoot. Drapes, or even more furniture, would help to defuse the sound of the man's footsteps, but nothing covered up the two large windows and the only furniture was a large wooden desk and the high-backed chair behind it.

The heavyset man sitting behind the desk didn't bother looking up from sorting the stacks of cash in front of him. "This better be important, Mugsy. I'm kinda busy here."

"We got a few new girls in, they're waiting for you to check 'em out. Seem like nice broads to me," Mugsy stated.

Boss Dogg sat back in his chair, chewing on the cigar in his mouth, his heavy jowls hanging on either side of his face. "And you decided that they couldn't wait? I thought I told you that I didn't want to be bothered."

"Yeah, you did, but…." Mugsy scratched the back of his head, causing his already impressive arm to swell in size. "Okay, maybe I shoulda waited, but they are out there, Boss, and they are a set of dolls, I tell ya."

"Waitresses, Mugsy. Don't think of them as anything else. That's what we hire them as, after all." He stood up, surprisingly not gaining much height, and walked around to stand by the considerably larger man. "How many times are we gonna have to have this talk, Mugsy? I count on you to be my first line. The man who handles everything that goes on outside this office for me. When you do that, it makes it easier for me to handle things back here. Back here is where the money happens, and we like money, don't we, Mugsy?"

"Yeah, Boss," Mugsy nodded enthusiastically.

"And how are we going to make money?" Boss asked.

Mugsy paused. "By finding new waitresses?"

It took longer than it should have for Boss Dogg to remove the cigar from his mouth. "No, Mugsy. We make money by being successful. Waitresses are good, they keep the club going and the customers happy, but they aren't the key to success. The key to success is one thing and one thing only: power."

"Oh! Yeah, you've said that before, Boss," Mugsy agreed.

"Good! You're learning." Boss pointed at Mugsy with the cigar. "Now, the key to power is making everyone think that you have it! And that means that the boss—which would be me in this case—has to look like the boss. Are you following, Mugsy?"

"Yeah," he nodded again. "Yeah, I am, Boss."

"Good!" Boss placed his arm on Mugsy's shoulder and walked the both of them towards the door. "So, you'll understand then when I tell you that, in order to continue to hold my position of power in the view of the young ladies outside," the volume of his voice steadily increased, "it is not their decision when I come see them, it's mine!"

Stopping at the door, Boss Dogg flung it open, shouting as he pointed out it. "Go tell those broads that I will come see them when I'm ready, and not a minute sooner, got it?"

Mugsy didn't move. He stood staring out the door, while Boss Dogg glared up at him.

"Aw, Boss," Mugsy groaned, "we got other problems, now."

With a jerk, Boss Dogg turned to look past the door. He did not see the half dozen or so prospective young employees that Mugsy suggested, but instead a solitary blond woman, sitting quietly at one of his tables. Her legs were crossed, with the upper foot dangling a shoe loosely from it. A tall flute of champagne rested in her hand, with an open bottle nearby on the table. A small clutch purse sat next to the bottle.

"Hello, Boss. I hope you don't mind that I let myself in," Pussy Katnip stated.

"How did you get in here!" Boss Dogg shouted as he stomped into the room.

"Side door." Pussy gestured vaguely. "It was unlocked, so I promise that I didn't break anything."

With Mugsy just behind him, Boss Dogg moved to loom over the seated woman, standing back on his heels and putting his hands on his hips. "And just where are my girls?"

"Your girls?" Pussy gently sat the glass down beside the bottle. "If you mean the group of lovely young women that were here when I arrived, I'm afraid they left."

"And just where did they go?" he huffed.

"The Kit Kat Klub. I offered them jobs," she answered.

At a glance, it appeared as though steam was rising from Boss Dogg's head, until the glow of his cigar revealed it as smoke.

"Ya want me to get her outta here, Boss?" Mugsy stepped forward, cracking his knuckles.

With a raise of his hand, Boss stopped Mugsy cold. "Actually, I want Miss Katnip to tell me why she's over here in the first place."

"I'm glad you asked." Pussy slid her chair back and stood gracefully. "Do you know a man named Todd Crocker?"

"Crocker? Crocker?" He rocked in place. "Yeah, I remember him. A business associate. What's it to you?"

"Business associate? I was under the impression that he worked at the water plant." A single eyebrow went up.

"Well, he doesn't work for me, we've just made a business deal," he explained.

"Oh good. He doesn't want to be a part of that agreement anymore," Pussy said.

"What? Heh, well, it ain't that easy," Boss laughed. "Y'see, he owes me money."

"Odd, that's not how he explains it. He says that he's already paid you off." Pussy walked to the back of the chair, her fingers lingering on the edge of it the whole way. "In fact, he says he paid you off early."

"Ah, well, he failed to mention the emergency clause. Matters beyond our control came into play and his deadline was moved up a bit. Sadly, he missed it." Boss pulled the cigar from his mouth.

"Did he? Well, how much does he owe?" she asked.

"Five hundred at the moment," Boss said.

Pussy blinked. "Five hundred? That's a good deal of money for just missing a due date."

"Well, that's the cost of doing business," he explained.

Her fingers strummed against the chair. "I see. Well, why don't I just pay you that and we'll call his debt clear?"

"Oh sure," Boss answered. "You can clear his debt right out... for five thousand."

She waited a heartbeat. "I'm sorry? That's not what you said."

"That is what the boss said!" Mugsy took a half step forward.

"Mugsy...." Boss' voice pulled the big man back. "Y'see, Pussy, you activated the outside interference clause. It upped his debt considerably."

Pussy let her eyes wander away from Boss Dogg, pausing for just a moment on Mugsy before scanning the rest of the room. It was about half the size of the Kit Kat Klub, with a large stage on the far side of the room, barely visible from the poor lighting. A wide central aisle was flanked by several round tables with mismatched chairs.

"Boss, how long have we known each other?" Pussy asked.

He put his cigar back in his mouth. "Since you moved in across the street seven years ago. You know that!"

"I do, but I wanted to make sure you remembered." Both of her hands slipped to the sides of the chair. "And in that time, how many times have I asked you for a favor?"

Boss Dogg's eyes closed slightly. "Never. Why?"

"Then why don't we see this as a first. Do me a favor and let Mr. Crocker's debt pass. Consider it paid in full. That way you avoid any added expense," she said.

"What expense?" he asked.

"The cost of replacing furniture." Her hands rubbed over the back of the chair. "We don't want to see your club to go downhill, now do we?"

"Downhill? The Dogg House is the finest club in Mutt Town!" Boss Dogg's pushed his chest out as far as possible.

"But Boss, the Kit Kat gets a lot more—"

"Shut it, Mugsy!" Boss shouted. "And get her outta my club!"

"You got it, Boss!" Mugsy's thin face grew wider with the snarl he put on it. "Time to go, Katnip."

"Now Mugsy, do we really want to go down this path again?" Pussy purred.

"You ain't gonna get me this time!" Mugsy lunged towards her.

Faster than the eye could follow, Pussy grabbed the chair and raised it up, smashing it against the brute attacking her. Splinters of wood showered down as Mugsy flew up into the air, landing hard on the ground.

She was on him instantly. Grabbing him by the shirt, she spun around, flinging him over ten feet into the seating area. The table and chairs he met did not respond well, and the sound of cracking wood filled the space.

Pussy looked to Boss. "Don't move." He didn't.

Five long strides brought Pussy to the damage, just as Mugsy was digging himself out of the mess. As he rose up, he brought the leg of a table with him.

20

"Now, Mugsy, let's not make this personal," Pussy took a step backwards.

He growled something unintelligible as he took a wild swing at Pussy. A quick leap backwards had the attack meet only air, but he pressed his slight advantage and continued forward, arm arcing widely with each step. Each swing pushed Pussy farther back, until she found the side of a table with her back. Her hand hit the surface of the table, landing on a heavy ashtray, which she then grasped. With a flick of her elbow and wrist it flung out, flying like a balanced toy. It struck Mugsy square in the nose, causing him to stagger backwards and drop the chair leg from his hand as he reached for the broken, bleeding protrusion.

Pussy stepped in before the wood had even reached the floor. Her left fist drove into Mugsy's stomach, forcing all the air out of him. As he doubled over her right fist came up, landing squarely with his chin. Mugsy lifted up off the floor, and once he hit the ground this time, he stayed down.

She stood over him, waiting a few seconds to make sure.

"Well," Pussy said calmly as she turned back to Boss Dogg, "that wasn't good for the decor. Now, can we get back to Mr. Crocker's situation?"

Rivulets of sweat ran down the fat man's face, and the only sound that came from him was a hard swallow.

Pussy walked over to her clutch and retrieved it. As she walked up to him, she pulled something out of the clutch.

"Here's what's going to happen. You're going to drop everything that Mr. Crocker owes you. You aren't going to bother him, or even remember that he exists. Your dealings with him are through. Am I clear?" She stopped inches away from him.

"Yeah. Yeah, sure." He nodded rapidly.

"Good." Her hand came up. Boss flinched. She stuffed a wad of cash into his breast pocket. "There's the five-hundred you originally said. You'll probably want to use it to clean this mess up."

With a spin on her heels, Pussy strode away, not giving another glance to the men behind her. It wasn't until the door behind her clicked shut that Boss Dogg finally moved.

"Lousy dame," he muttered. Then he pulled the cash from his breast pocket and quickly counted it before shoving it into his front pant pocket. "Mugsy!" he shouted, turning towards the damage. "Get up, ya bum!"

A low moan came up from the floor, but Mugsy barely moved at all. Boss Dogg prodded him with the tip of his shoe, but the big man barely moved.

"She has an impressive punch, don't you think?"

Boss Dogg jumped. The voice came from the shadows of the stage, low and smooth, soft and silky.

"Who's there!" he shouted as he stepped off to the side in an attempt to get a better look at the stage.

Slowly, a figure emerged from the shadows, melting out of the darkness and into the light. She was long and lush, wearing a red dress that hugged her body like a lover's passionate embrace. A shock of black hair curved over her face, hiding half of it from view, while the rest fell down past her shoulders. A single cold grey eye was visible above her left cheek and the beauty mark on it. With each alternate swaying step, a leg that could stop traffic displayed itself, and then hid itself completely when she came to a stop.

"I'm sorry." Something akin to a smile played along her lips. "I didn't mean to alarm you."

"I...I...I...." Boss Dogg stammered. His hand came up and adjusted his tie. "Who are you? What are you doing here?"

"Oh, I came here looking for you, actually." She turned and walked to the stairs, then descended them slowly. "I find myself in an unusual situation, and from everything that I've heard around town, you can help."

"Oh really?" Boss Dogg pulled down on his coat. "Well, young lady, there's very little that Boss Dogg can't handle!"

She strode towards him at a casual pace. "Except for Pussy Katnip, it seems."

"Oh, that...that was just a.... Don't you worry about Pussy Katnip!" He stepped over Mugsy and moved closer to the approaching woman. "What is it that I can do for you?"

"Actually, I want you to help me get a job." She sauntered up and saddled beside him. "A singing job."

"Uh, well, um, we could always use a talented performer here at my club," he managed to say eventually.

"Oh, not here. I want you to get me a job over at the Kit Kat Klub. I want to help you deal with Pussy Katnip and get her out of your hair once and for all." Her hand came up and brushed up and down the lapels of Boss' jacket.

To anyone watching, it looked as though the cigar slipped and fell from Boss Dogg's mouth in slow motion. His jaw dropped lower and lower until his mouth hung so open that it couldn't hold onto the cigar any longer. As it tumbled down his chest, Boss reacted, stepping backwards and brushing down his body. That's when his feet tangled over Mugsy's body lying behind him, and he stumbled and staggered backwards, eventually landing on his posterior.

The impact, combined with the tittering laughter above him, was enough to finally roust Mugsy, who sat up alarmed.

"Boss! You okay?" The continued laughter drew his attention the other way. He looked up at the woman standing nearby. "Whoa! Who's the dreamboat?"

"Don't worry, Mugsy," she chuckled, "I'm a friend. My name is Foxy. Foxy Kitt."

Red is the Darkest Color

Brett Brooks

Chapter Three

He saw her standing at the top of the stairs, surveying the club. Very few ever saw the Kit Kat Klub from her particular perspective, but then, very few were ever invited up to her private quarters. Many of the employees had been up to her office at the top of the stairs, but the number that actually went into her home could be counted on one hand. He was lucky enough to be in that group.

"Hello, Robert." She announced herself as she took her foot took her first step.

The back of his two forefingers touched the top of his head. "Good afternoon, Miss Katnip. How's things?"

"Everything is fine with me, Robert. How are you today?" She left the steps and immediately worked her way towards the bar. Her hand retrieved the stack of mail waiting for her and began to sort through it.

"Fit as a fiddle!" he chirped. "But, well, I do have bad news. We still haven't heard anything from Jenny."

Pussy's hands stopped moving. "Did you send anyone over to her place?"

He nodded before he spoke. "Yeah. It's clean. Like she beat feet and never even lived there. Place was perfect, Miss Katnip. No signs of funny business at all."

"Odd." She tapped the mail against the counter. "I wouldn't have thought she was the type. Shame. She had a real future here." Once more her attention returned to the mail, and a few letters in she stopped and pulled a single envelope free. He watched as she slipped her pinky into the edge of the letter and run the fingernail along the length. "Hmm."

"What is it, Miss Katnip?" Robby asked.

"Maybe our Jenny is responsible after all," she said. He saw a sparkle in her eyes as she looked over at him. It just wasn't about him, despite his best hopes. "Listen to this. 'Miss Katnip, I want to start by apologizing for not giving you this information in person. Everything happened so quickly that I just got the chance to send you this letter to give you this information. I think that I told you about my grandmother, and that she used to be a singer in Los Angeles. It turns out that she knows someone who knows someone, and, well, to make a long story short, she got me in a movie. I had to leave as soon as she called, in the middle of the night, so I couldn't tell you. I just got here and sent this out. I hope you understand. I will never forget my time at the Kit Kat. Thank you so much. Love, Jenny.'" She dropped the letter down and gave a slight twist to her head.

"Well, I guess it explains things, but," Robby shrugged, "I dunno, Miss Katnip, it doesn't seem too responsible to me. And not too much like Jenny, either."

"Oh, don't be mad, Robert. You can't blame the girl for taking the chance. If she wants to be on the silver screen, the only way is by going to Tinsel Town." Pussy took the rest of the mail and put it in a stack on the bar. "By the way, tables five, seven, eight, and twelve all are missing candles in their centerpiece. We need to get that taken care of before we open. And see what you can do about table six. That leg is still wobbling. If someone hit it hard enough it would collapse. We can't have that."

"I'll have the girls get on that right away," Robby answered.

"I appreciate that, Robert," Pussy answered. "I'm going to go check on the kitchen."

"Okay, I gotta finish getting today's shipment of hooch put out." His hand touched the closest of several boxes stacked beside him.

"It's not 'hooch,' Robert. We don't serve 'hooch' at the Kit Kat," she chuckled as she turned and walked towards the double doors leading out of the club proper and into the kitchen. Robby watched her until she was completely out of the room and then sunk beneath the bar to go back to work.

The clinking of the bottles drowned out the sound of the woman's heels as she walked into the room, so Robby heard nothing until she spoke.

"Hello?" Her voice stopped him immediately. "Is anyone here?"

Rising above the counter brought the unexpected visitor into view slowly. By the time he was fully standing his mouth hung open.

"Oh, hello." She wore scarlet. Deep enough color to match the sound of her voice and the shape of her body. "I didn't mean to startle you."

"You…uh, no, you didn't." Robby blinked a couple of times and managed to close his mouth before it went completely dry. "I'm sorry miss, but we're closed. Don't open for another couple of hours, yet."

"I wasn't here for a drink, handsome." A glint of light hit her one visible eye. "Actually, I was hoping that Miss Katnip might be available. Is she here?"

"She's, uh, she…why are you wanting to see Miss Katnip?" he asked.

"Oh, well, nothing I suppose. I probably shouldn't even have come here." She turned and took one step.

"No, wait!" Robby vaulted over the bar in a single bound. In a flash he was next to her. "I mean, I just need to tell her why you want to see her, that's all."

"If it's no trouble then, I was wanting to see Miss Katnip about a job," she said.

"A job? Well, we just hired a handful of waitresses the other day, so—"

"No," she interrupted, "I was wanting to audition to be a singer."

"Really? We did just lose a gal the other day, and it looks like she's gone with the wind, so you're timing's pretty good." He perked up. "I'll go let her know."

Her hand came out and grabbed his arm with the force of a feather. It froze him in place. "If you don't think it will bother her. I…well, Miss Katnip has quite the reputation, and I would hate to disappoint her."

"Aww, don't you fret, doll. Miss Katnip's about as nice as they come. She'll give you the straight scoop on what's what around here." He carefully put his hand over hers. "I'm sure you'll knock her out."

"Oh," she sighed, "I do hope you're right about that."

"Let me go get her. You want something to drink before I go?" he asked.

"No, thank you. You're far too kind, Mr....?"

"Byrd. Robert Byrd, but call me Robby. All my friends do." He gave her a smile. The smile.

"Thank you, Robby." Her eye closed halfway.

"Uh, you bet. Wait here, would ya?" He kept his head towards her as he took his first steps, which is likely what caused him to walk into the chair and send it clattering. He quickly gathered it up and put it back in place. With a slightly quicker step he moved towards the kitchen doors.

They opened from the other side before he got to them. Pussy Katnip stepped through them and immediately saw Robby.

"Robert, is everything all right? I heard a bit of a commotion."

"Yeah, yeah, Miss Katnip. Sorry, that was me bein' clumsy." He stepped to the side and pointed towards the bar and the woman standing beside it. "You, uh, you got someone here to see you."

"I see that," Pussy stated as she walked towards her new guest. Robby followed close behind. A moment before she got to her, Pussy spoke. "Good afternoon. How can I help you?"

"Just getting a chance to meet you in person is enough, but, well, I was actually hoping to possibly get a job," she answered.

"What kind of job?" Pussy asked.

"I'm a singer. I was hoping you'd give me a chance to show you what I can do," she said.

"I don't see why not." She extended her hand. "I'm Pussy Katnip."

The other woman took her hand. "It's a pleasure to meet you face-to-face, Miss Katnip. I'm Foxy Kitt."

"Miss Kitt." Pussy shook her hand.

"Call me Foxy, please," she said as she pulled her hand back.

"All right, Foxy. Well, I'm sorry to say that the band isn't in yet. They don't show up until just before opening usually," Pussy explained. "So, I'm not sure what to tell you about singing for me."

"Actually, I'd love to show you what I can do all by myself, Miss Katnip," Foxy purred. "If that's okay with you, that is."

"A cappella it is, then." Pussy took a step back and gestured towards the stage. Foxy took the direction, and Pussy followed in behind her after a brief delay. "Do you have any experience, Foxy?"

Moving slowly behind them, Robby kept close, but not too close. This wasn't his place to be, but it would have been easier to give a rabid dog a root canal than take his eyes off of them right now.

"Oh, I'm very experienced," Foxy turned to look over her shoulder, "but this would be my first singing job."

Pussy laughed and stopped at a table a couple back from the stage. "The stairs are on the left. Go on up and then whenever you're ready...."

With a short nod, Foxy turned away and went around the stage and up the stairs. Pussy took a seat at the table, pushing the chair back so she could lounge casually.

Foxy moved from the back of the stage towards the microphone at the front at a casual pace, to say the least. Every step brought her further into the stage lights, and those lights did their very best to show what she had to offer.

"Whew," Robby barely muttered. "That is one swell dish."

Barely turning her head, Pussy spoke just loud enough for him to hear, "Why don't you go back to the bar, Robert? Sounds like you need to stand behind something right now."

"Uh, sure thing, Miss Katnip." He took a few steps back, but not as far as the bar. "You bet. I'll be…just back here."

Robby swore he heard Pussy chuckle before she turned back to the stage. Foxy was standing at the microphone. Her left hand rested alongside the stand, slowly working it's way up to the squarish mic itself. She stood close enough that the mic stand pushed into her dress and body beneath it. Slowly, she brought her right hand up and brushed it along her hair, barely revealing the right side of her face. A second time brought her right eye into view for the first time. It seemed to Robby to be focused directly on Pussy's face.

Foxy took a deep breath, and then a voice like mahogany silk filled the room.

> *I give you lovin' all the time,*
> *Night and day, I'm the gal,*
> *To grant your wishes, so sublime,*
> *But late last night in my locale,*
> *I couldn't help but think…*
>
> *What will you do for me?*
> *How can you help me see,*
> *Why I shouldn't go away,*
> *Give what I've got every day,*
> *To someone in the pink?*

What will you do for me?
How could you let me be,
All alone, by myself,
All my gifts up on a shelf,
Just waiting on the brink.

What will you do for me?
Could you just set me free?
Look upon me and perceive,
What's resting right up my sleeve,
For you to take a drink.

The time is here, I must confess,
To end my song and honest plea.
So I'll just slip off my new dress,
And then I think you'll see,
That you'll do anything for me.

Can you doubt that in a blink,
That you'll do anything for me?

The last note resonated through the club, and as Foxy ended her song, her mouth hung slightly open. It mirrored the expression of almost everyone else in the club—almost. Applause broke out from the gathered staff, who had heard Foxy's siren call and left their post to find her. Robby was right there with them, and it wasn't until he felt the cool air on his tongue that he realized he was one of the staff holding his mouth open.

Whether from curiosity or just a desire to see if his opinion was shared, he looked at the table nearby. Pussy sat silently, legs crossed and hand resting gently on her own knee. She was staring straight up at Foxy, and the woman on stage was looking right back at her. After a moment he saw Pussy glance to the side of the stage.

Reading her intent, Foxy let her hand slip from the microphone and moved towards the stairs. By the time she reached the bottom of the stairs, Pussy had moved to meet her.

"Well?" Foxy purred.

"Well what?" Pussy questioned back.

"What do you think of me?" Foxy's voice was soft and low.

"I think that you have a very impressive," he saw Pussy's eyes wander for a moment, "set of pipes."

"Thank you. Coming from you, that's quite a compliment." A slow blink accompanied Foxy's words.

"This isn't an easy job," Pussy stated. "It takes commitment and hard work. Are you willing to put that in?"

"I'm willing to put in anything you ask. I'm not afraid of any sort of job," Foxy answered.

"I see." The two women stood five feet away from each other. Just enough space to keep them apart.

The shadows of the room came up and around them both as the lights on the stage went dim. Robby lost sight of them for a moment as his eyes adjusted to see the women in this new light.

"How soon can you start?" Pussy asked.

"When do you want me?" Foxy replied.

A brief pause filled the space.

"You go on at eight tonight. Ask for Robin. She'll help you get set up with a station backstage. I'll get the band in a little early so you can go over a set with them." Pussy extended her hand.

"Welcome to the Kit Kat Klub, Miss Kitt."

She took the offered hand. "I told you, please call me Foxy."

"I remember." Pussy shook her hand gently. "It's going to be a packed house tonight. Good night to start."

"If you say so, Miss Katnip. I'm just here to do what you say." She slipped her hand free. Robby noticed she let her fingers trail along Pussy's palm.

"Then do what you did on the stage a few minutes ago," Pussy said. "Now, if you'll excuse me, I have some things I need to do."

She stepped away, and Foxy followed her along for a few steps. Pussy turned to head upstairs, with Foxy moving the other way, towards the bar.

"Holy mackerel!" Robby ran up to her before she got all the way there. "That was swell, Foxy!"

"Thank you, Robby. I do hope that Miss Katnip was impressed." Her dress barely moved as she slipped onto a stool.

"I'll say!" he stated with a short swallow.

Foxy glanced over at the young lady nearby.

"Oh, Foxy, let me introduce my kid sister, Robin," Robby said with a gesture. "Robin, this is Foxy Kitt."

"Gosh, Foxy, that was about as good as Miss Katnip herself," Robin said.

"Do you really think so, Robin?" Foxy asked.

"You bet! It was the cat's meow!" Robin answered.

"You're very kind, Robin." Foxy closed her eyes for a moment.

"Robin's a good egg, Foxy. She wouldn't lie," Robby explained.

"That reminds me, Robin. Miss Katnip told me you might help me get set up in the back," Foxy stood up and let her hands move down her body, straightening out her dress. "Do you think you could help me out?"

"S-sure. I'd be happy to," Robin replied. "Just follow me."

Foxy looked over the bar. "I'll see you later, Robby."

"I hope so," he answered. "Break a leg tonight, Foxy!"

"I hope I will, Robby," she answered.

"Don't worry, Robby," Robin added. "She's gonna do great!"

"You know," Foxy smiled, "I agree. I think this experience is going to be great."

Brett Brooks

Chapter Four

The club was packed. That wouldn't be unusual for a Friday
or Saturday, but, to the best of his knowledge, this never
happened on a Tuesday. George stood at the cusp of the main
room, using the slight elevation of the stairs to see out over the
floor in an attempt to get his bearings. In the far right corner,
not exactly close to the stage and definitely a good distance
from the band, sat two couples. They were talking, laughing,
and sharing some drinks. Nothing unusual about it, except
for the fact that he always thought of that as the empty seat he
could always count on when he walked into the club. It was his
table. His shoulders rolled, and his eyes narrowed, eventually
moving on to the rest of the room. Everywhere they fell, he saw
the same thing: a table full of people.

He finally decided to make his way to the only seat available at
the far end of the bar.

"Chief!" Robby shouted just loud enough to be heard over the
combined din of the band and crowd. George lifted his right
hand up and touched a pair of fingers to his forehead in a near-
salute. "Been a while. What's cooking with you, friend?"

"Hi, Robby," George took off his hat and smoothed back his
short brown hair. His long ears hung down on either side of his

head, giving a gentle look to his canine features. He set his hat on the bar and immediately his fingers began to play along the brim. "Can you set me up with two fingers?"

"You bet, Chief."

Less than twenty seconds passed before there was a glass on the bar. Five seconds later half of its contents were gone. "So," George swallowed again, clearing his throat silently, "what's the hubbub? I thought Tuesdays were quiet around here."

"They were, yeah," Robby leaned his hands on the bar. "That was before."

"Before what?" George asked.

Robby laughed. "You'll see, Chief."

"Okay," George dragged the word out as long as two syllables allowed. "Is Pussy around?"

"Miss Katnip just went into the back. I can go let her know you're here if you want," Robby explained.

"No, that's all right. I don't want to upset her. If she's busy tonight—"

"If she finds out you were here and I didn't tell her, thing is, she's gonna be way more upset with me than if I interrupt something else." Robby tossed a towel over his shoulder and started to walk away. "I'll be right back."

"No, Robby, don't." George raised a hand, stopping the bartender. "She'll come back out. I'll talk to her then. I'm not going anywhere."

His foot took another half step before the rest of him pulled back to the bar. "I ain't gonna argue with you, Chief." He pulled the towel off his shoulder and began to wipe down a glass. "But, hey, where have you been, anyway?"

"The Chief in Big City got married, and they asked if I could fill in for him while he was on his honeymoon." The aroma of countless forms of alcohol wafted over from behind the bar, pushed on by the motion of the towel, stinging George's sensitive nose. "Pussy knew where I was."

"Gotcha." The glass clinked against its neighbor as Robby put it back in place. The sound was enhanced by the fact that the band went silent at the same moment. For a brief second there was a hush through the room, which was drowned out by a soft murmur as realization sank in.

A male voice came over the sound system. "Ladies and gentleman, The Kit Kat Klub is proud to present, Miss Foxy Kitt!"

A roar of applause erupted from almost everyone in the place. George raised an eyebrow.

"Foxy Kitt?" He turned to Robby. "Why isn't Pussy coming out first?"

"Just watch." Robby nodded towards the stage, and George followed.

The woman standing in the spotlight raised her head slightly, singing up into the microphone. The words rose up even higher, filling the entire room and falling down upon George's ears. He sat there, his mouth hanging slightly, unbeknownst to him.

"What's the matter?" George almost jumped off his chair. "Cat got your tongue?"

"Pussy!" He hugged the feline, her form molding to his perfectly. "Sorry I didn't hear you...I mean, I...."

"I know exactly what you mean." He saw her look past him to the stage. "She's pretty damn captivating."

"I'll say," he muttered. "Where did you find her?"

"She found me, believe it or not." Pussy pointed to Robby, and then gestured to the bar. "It was quite the coup, too. You remember Jenny? She got a break and headed out to Tinsel Town to try to make it on the silver screen."

"What?" Another glass was placed beside George, and then another beside Pussy. "When did the new girl start?"

"Almost two weeks ago now. Just after you headed out to Big City." She picked up the glass and threw the whole contents down in a single slug. A few drops tried to sneak down her lips, but her tongue came out and captured them immediately.

"That can't be right. I saw Jenny just two days ago." George pulled the glass over to the edge of the bar, but didn't lift it up.

"Two days? That's not possible." Pussy turned her right shoulder away from him. "She sent me a letter. It was post-marked from Tinsel Town. She apologized for leaving."

"I'm not saying you didn't get a letter," he picked up his drink and took a small sip, "but she was in Big City. I saw her walking down the street."

He noticed her rubbing her two forefingers against her thumb on her left hand. "You're sure it was her?"

"She was in a bit of a rush, but yeah, I'd put some money on it." He set the drink back down and leaned towards Pussy. "It was her."

Pussy said nothing back to him. Body language spoke volumes, though, with narrow eyes and tight lips.

"What are you thinking?" he asked.

"That I need to take a trip to Big City." Her voice had changed, dropping down an octave. George recognized it too well. Raising her hand to call Robby over was more proof.

"Robert, I'm going to be leaving town for a few days. I'm putting you in charge of the club," Pussy explained.

"Out of town? What's the low down, Miss Katnip? You okay?"

George saw a glint in Pussy's eyes as she answered. "Nothing to worry about, Robert. Just something I need to check on. And I won't leave until tomorrow morning, which will give us time to get things set up tonight."

The din of the room increased, and George saw Foxy Kitt taking a bow on stage. He turned towards Pussy before she got his attention.

"I have to go, George." Her hands came out, and he took it as an invite to take them into his. "It was great seeing you. Stay as long as you like, but I'm afraid I might not be able to come back and visit tonight. Don't worry about the bill, it's on me."

"You don't have to—"

She cut him off with a single finger to his lips. "I know, but I'm going to."

"Do you need me to come with you, Pussy?" She pulled the finger back.

"No, I can handle this. Just tell me what street you saw Jenny on, if you can."

He could, and he did. "She was on 4th, crossing over Duncan. Heading east, if I remember correctly."

The applause was just beginning to fade in the background. "I've got to go. Foxy may be a hot commodity, but I still have to put some time in on stage myself."

"Break a leg, Pussy." He stayed still, watching her walk away. Peeking up over her left shoulder, the fingers of her right hand waved at him. At least, he hoped it was at him as he settled back onto his seat beside the bar.

"You know what that's about, Chief?"

"I do, Robby," he answered, "at least, in part. I'm not exactly sure what's going on, though. And knowing Pussy, it's best if she tells you."

"Is it bad?" There was a hint of concern behind the curiosity of Robby's voice.

George drained the glass dry. "I suppose that's what Pussy is going to find out."

"Are you gonna go with her?" Robby leaned in against the bar.

"She didn't ask me to." George pushed the glass towards him in suggestion.

Robby didn't miss the hint, and he spun around right in George's view. He turned around so quickly that it seemed impossible for him to have done anything but spin, but when he faced George again he had a bottle in his hand. He poured as he spoke. "But if she's going to be in trouble, you might oughta go, Chief. She might need you."

"Do you really think so, Robby?" George mindlessly tapped one finger on the bar.

"You bet I do! And I don't mind telling you to go. I'd be in cahoots with Boss Dogg if I thought it would help out Miss Katnip."

"That's not what I meant, Robby," George said. "I meant do you really think that she needs anyone? Pussy is the most capable person that I've ever met. She's saved me several times, but I can't think of a single time that I've returned that favor."

"Oh, c'mon, Chief! I've seen you help out Miss Katnip plenty of times!" If they were closer, George got the feeling that he would have received a chuck on the shoulder with that sentence.

"I'm always glad to help Pussy out, Robby, but that doesn't mean that she needs me," George said. "That woman doesn't need anyone, and you know it."

"What a shame." The deep voice caught George's attention in an instant.

She stood there, shoulder down and hip up, looking right at him. George stared. He didn't mean to, and he was aware of it, but he couldn't turn himself away. Her one visible eye had already caught him, and he wasn't pulling away. Part of him didn't even want to try.

"I think any woman would be thrilled to get help from a man like you," Foxy purred.

"Well, I, uh, wouldn't want to force anything on anyone," George answered, "especially not a beautiful woman."

"Oh please. Sometimes a woman wants to have things forced upon her." Foxy's lips stayed slightly open, her fangs just peeking from beneath her lips.

"I would never presume something like that," George answered.

Foxy's eye shifted to the empty stool beside him. "May I?"

Immediately, George stood up. "Of course!" He pulled the stool out slightly, readying it.

"Thank you." Foxy moved to George's side of the chair, passing close enough to brush her dress against his jacket. He picked up the scent of cardamom and patchouli as her hair turned away from him.

She settled onto the chair, and then her legs moved, and he watched her dress fall away, leaving a long, silky display. Her hand came out, pulling his eyes up above her waist.

"Foxy Kitt." She held the hand out, palm down, fingers dangling.

"I…heard your performance." He took her hand and held it for a moment. "You're very talented."

"That's very kind of you, Mr…?"

"Oh! I'm sorry. Yeah, I'm George Pup. Chief George Pup of the Mutt Town Fire Department. It's a pleasure to meet you." He nodded to complete his sentence.

He felt her hand slip from his fingers. "So, did you enjoy it?"

The words stayed in his ears for a moment. "I'm sorry, what are you…?" He almost smacked himself on the head. "Oh! Yes, yes I enjoyed your singing very much. As I said, you're very talented."

Her eyelid fluttered at him. "Then why weren't you watching me?"

"I beg your pardon?" He heard her clearly the first time, but the question gave him a moment's pause. "Oh, it's because I was with Pussy. Miss Katnip. We were catching up. I've been out of town for a while."

"Oh." Her head lowered just enough to take her eye to the floor. "I understand. Miss Katnip is quite the woman. I can see why you would prefer her over me."

"What?" A quick shudder ran over his face. "I didn't.... Miss Katnip and I are old friends. It had nothing to do with you."

"Promise?" In a flash her head came back up, and George felt her stare into him.

"Don't be so insecure, Miss Kitt."

"Foxy. Please, call me Foxy," she corrected before he could get out another word.

"All right, Foxy, don't be so harsh. From what I've seen here tonight, you have quite a talent, and, I have to say, are quite the attractive woman." George tried to keep his eyes from wandering. The image of her bared legs still burned in his mind. "You have nothing to worry about."

"Oh, George...." Her hand came out and touched his. "It is all right that I call you George, isn't it?"

"Of course." No attempt was made to remove her hand from his.

"You are so kind." He watched the corner of her lip play up. "Miss Katnip has been amazing—taking me in, guiding me along, giving me a new direction—but it's difficult to live in her shadow. Hearing someone like you say kind things like that means so much to me."

"I...I just was telling you...." He looked down just as she squeezed his hand. "You're welcome."

Once again he felt her pull her hand away, but this time there was the faint sensation of her fingernails dragging against the back of his hand. "I wish I could properly thank you. Miss Katnip is so lucky, having a man like you to take care of her."

"I don't take care of Pussy," George answered. "She really doesn't need me to take care of her. That's what I was talking to Robby about," he turned to discover that Robby was nowhere to be found, "well, what we were talking about when you walked up."

"Oh, I see." She uncrossed and recrossed her legs. George kept his eyes north of her shoulders, but his peripheral vision caught a hint of the show. "I would have thought you quite capable of taking care of Pussy."

With a little effort, he fought down his first response. "I help her out when she needs it, but, like I said, Miss Katnip is very capable."

"Well, I don't suppose," she moved in, and George suddenly noticed how hot they were keeping the club these days, "that since you aren't taking care of her, that maybe I could talk you into…me?"

He coughed. "What?"

She laughed. "I suppose that I was wondering what it would take to get a guy like you to ask out a gal like me?"

George sat back on his stool. "Uh, that's a very intriguing question, Foxy, but I have to say that, well, I'm not really looking for something like that right now."

Foxy leaned away and arched her back just as the air conditioning kicked in, from what George could tell. "Not looking, or just ignoring it? Maybe because you already have plans for someone else?"

"I told you," George said slowly, "Pussy and I are just friends, if that's what you're implying."

"I'm not implying anything, George. I'm just a little jealous, is all." George caught a glint in her eye as she spoke.

Music swelled through the room once more, and again a male voice sounded through the speakers. "Ladies and gentlemen, the Kit Kat Klub is proud to welcome back to the stage, the one, the only," the announcer paused for effect, "Pussy Katnip!"

The room roared as Pussy walked out onto stage.

"Well, I suppose I should be going." Foxy slipped from the stool, and George rose from his at the same time, bringing the two of them practically into contact with each other. George felt her breath on his cheek. "I don't think it's a good idea for me to be out here when Miss Katnip performs. I don't want anything to distract from her singing."

"Well, uh, it was very nice meeting you, Foxy." George's attempt to pull away was thwarted by the stool grinding into his backside.

"The pleasure was all mine, George." Somehow, she took a half-step towards him, and George suddenly found himself sitting back on his stool. "I do hope to see much more of you in the future." She leaned in, and with nowhere left to go, George felt her press against him. Her lips planted on his cheek, parting with a faint smacking sound. "I hope you have a pleasant evening."

"Yes." His voice cracked, followed by a cough. "Yes, thank you. It's already been very…nice."

Not another word was spoken. He watched her walk away, up to the point where the sound of a song finally came through. Turning back to the stage, he saw Pussy up there in mid-song. How had he missed the first half of it?

Still, after only a few seconds, he found himself moving, leaning into the bar. Every thing she did on stage, every motion, was followed not only by him, but by everyone in the room. He marveled at her.

Foxy might have controlled the room when she performed, but Pussy, she owned the place.

Red is the Darkest Color

Brett Brooks

Chapter Five

"Miss Katnip! Welcome back!"

Pussy took off her gloves and carried them in her left hand.
The thick air of Big City hit her as she stepped clear of the car.
The familiar smell was like no other place she had ever been.
It was like a perfume of oil, garbage, and concrete. She did her
best not to breathe it in.

"Thank you…Phillip." The young man's face was familiar, but
the name was only vague. She watched his face for any sign
that she got the name wrong.

"It's wonderful to see you again. It's been a while." He closed
the door to the car without hesitation, and Pussy relaxed.

"Yes, sadly. How have things been?" Pussy waited for Phillip to
pull her bags from the trunk.

"You know what they say about life in Big City. There's always
something going on." He closed the trunk and tapped on the
fender a couple of times, signaling the driver.

"So, what is going on? Anything happening I should know
about?" Pussy followed Phillip as he walked towards the
entrance of the hotel, pushing the cart carrying her belongings.

"There's a great show that opened up down at the Limelight Club." He laughed after his statement. "Aw heck, why am I telling you that? You probably know everyone working the show already."

"Actually, that's good to know. I was here looking for a singer, myself. I'll be sure to check it out." She pulled out her bag and opened it. She moved the small bottle of red liquid to the side, and pulled out a couple of ones, handing them to Phillip. "Thanks."

"Thank you, Miss Katnip!" He tipped his hat towards her. "Just let me know if there's anything else that I can do for you."

The moment that she stepped into the lobby, Pussy noticed the noise of the city outside by its sudden absence. The din of car horns and traffic faded away, leaving a pleasant near silence. She could even hear her own heels clicking against the marble floor as she walked to the front desk.

"Miss Katnip! Welcome back to the Fountain Royale. It's wonderful to see you again."

Pussy remembered her clearly. Olive Green, the delightful young lizard lady who moved her way up from house cleaner to behind the desk, and from what the badge on her chest indicated, she had made it all the way up to assistant manager.

"I could say the same about you, Olive. I'm glad to see you're still here."

"Oh, the Royale is my home. I don't think I could ever leave." Her hands shuffled along the desk, bringing over the register. "Are you checking in?"

"I am." Pussy nodded.

"For how many nights?" Olive brought her pen to the register, waiting for Pussy to respond.

"I'm not sure, actually. I imagine two at least, but I can't say beyond that. Is that going to be a problem?"

"Of course not." Olive wrote something into the book in front of her. "I'll mark you down as indefinite. Don't worry about it. It's mostly just for book keeping, anyway. Would you like a single room?"

"Would you check to see if a suite is available?" Pussy moved her eyes down to the register before Olive gave a reply.

"Let me check." Her fingers began flipping the pages, just as Pussy knew she would.

Olive's finger ran down along the side of the register pages, providing a guide not only for her, but for Pussy to read what was written along each line. Pussy was looking for a name, any familiar name at all. She wasn't that surprised to find one.

"We do, actually." Olive looked back up, and Pussy moved her eyes to meet the attractive young lizard. "Would you like me to book you into one?"

"That would be wonderful, thank you," Pussy replied.

"Great!" Olive quickly filled out the page, and then put it on the counter, facing towards Pussy. "If you could sign here, please?"

With a slight flourish, Pussy put her name in the book, and took that opportunity to confirm the name that she saw before. Room 811, with a check-in date of yesterday. Timing was off, but the name was dead on.

"Okay, here's your key. You're in room 1128. I'll have your bags sent up right away. Enjoy your stay, Miss Katnip."

"I hope to." Gently, Pussy took the key and stepped away towards the elevator, passing up the staircase. After the ride up, she made her way down the hall. Her room was directly across from the upper end of the staircase that spiraled down through the center of the hotel to the lobby far below.

The door unlocked and opened easily. Moving straight through to the far side, Pussy looked out the windows, confirming her position in the hotel and getting a lay of the current state of the roads below. Busy, but nothing beyond normal. Popping into the bedroom, she flopped down on the bed, sinking into the soft mattress. With a little hesitance, she sat up and looked around the room. Her shoes slipped off easily, dangling on her toes for a moment before she let them drop to the floor. Her toes stretched out as she let out a short sigh.

A glance to her right located her handbag. Pussy reached in and carefully pulled out the small bottle, setting it on the bedside table. Her bare feet padded across the carpet, enjoying the feel of it as she gathered up the glass she spotted on the table in the sitting area and returning to the bed with it.

This time she stood, picking up the bottle she placed, and swirling the contents gently. "I have the sneaking suspicion I'm going to need this."

The bottle clinked against the edge of the glass, and the red liquid poured out a double shot. Despite the familiarity, her nose still wrinkled at the smell as it came closer to her mouth. Throwing back her head, she tossed the drink down her throat. Quickly, she set the glass down, just barely in time.

A jolt of electricity shot through her, causing her to convulse and fall over onto the bed. All of the earlier comfort she felt from the bed was gone. Each spasm was another experience between agony and ecstasy, taking her to the brink of her physical limits.

Suddenly, the room spun away, and visions of faces washed over her mind. George. Foxy. Her mother. And a woman she had never seen before. The Kit Kat Klub was awash in red, deep and dark. Cold and heat both stabbed at her nerves. Isolation from everything. And then blackness.

The first thing she noticed as her senses returned was the intensity of her breathing. As she brought her breath under control, she became aware of the cold sweat that left her fur slightly damp.

"Damn," she whispered. Every time was a new experience. Some severe, some minor. None of them lasting more than a second or two, no matter how long it seemed to her.

There was a noise. Something coming from the other part of the room. The door. Someone was knocking on the door.

Slipping her shoes back on, Pussy stood and straightened her dress before walking into the other part of her suite. She made her way to the window, and turned to face the door.

"It's unlocked," she announced.

The door swung in with a gentle squeak, all but drowned out by the sound of the bad wheel on the cart carrying the luggage. A large man with equine features in an ill-fitting uniform pushed the carrier into the room, pausing to close the door after he passed through it.

"Good morning, Miss." His voice was rough, but friendly. "Where would you like me to place your bags?"

Pussy did a quick eye count, confirming the five bags—two large and three small—that she brought with her. "Just go ahead and place them in the bedroom, please."

She saw his head bob slightly and resume moving the carrier. He passed her by and moved into the room.

"Just set them beside the bed." She moved past him, remembering that her clutch was on the bed already. "I'll unpack them in—"

The blow to the back of her head sent her reeling. She tumbled head over heels, finding herself sprawled out beside the bed. Flashes of light filled her field of vision. She was all but blind, but she still was planning her next four actions.

She rolled beneath the bed. It was a tight squeeze, but she'd been in tighter. Coming out the other side she pulled off her shoes, counting in her head. Three seconds she figured. Turned out to be two.

As the man rounded the bed she threw the shoe upwards, catching him in the face. Her hands went beside her head and she sprung up to her feet with a flip. This time she saw his hand, and the blackjack it held. Ducking beneath it, she rolled over the bed, coming back to her feet on the far side of it.

He was moving towards her again, lunging almost. Shifting her body weight to her left, she let him slide very close before bringing her right fist up into his gut. The sound of air pushing out of his lungs was clear, but the big man didn't double over as she expected. Instead his elbow came up, driving into her side. She felt her feet come up off the ground as she was thrown up and back into the wall beside the door. Using the opportunity, she twisted and slipped out of the door and into the adjoining room.

Scrambling backwards she pushed towards the windows just as he came after her. Every one of her senses focused in on him. The sound of his breath was slightly labored. There was a faint smell of fear mixed with alcohol coming off of him. And, most importantly she thought, he had an almost imperceptible limp with his right leg.

A nearby lamp sufficed for an impromptu weapon, which she grabbed as she ducked below his arcing swing. The sound of the lamp breaking over the man's knee hid the sound of his own knee suffering worse damage.

He dropped down as she stood up. Her left hand grabbed the lapel of his jacket and her right came towards his jaw. She gripped harder as she felt him start to slip away from the force of her blow, pulling him back up towards her as her fist came down a second time. This time, she let go, and he fell to the ground like a bag of meat.

Pussy stepped back, waiting to make sure he didn't move. Three seconds later she shook her head, trying to clear the buzzing cobwebs that still lingered. Her hand came up to her face, and when it pulled back she saw a stain of red on her fingers. She tasted blood on her lip. No doubt split open when she hit her head.

Pushing past him, Pussy went into the bedroom. A dull thud softened by the carpet came from her unceremoniously tossing the luggage onto the floor. Taking the now empty cart back into the other room, she pulled the man up onto it. He was heavy. Dense muscle covered every inch of him.

Something about his face was familiar. It took her almost five seconds to recognize him. "Fred 'Ironhoof' Trotter," she muttered. She saw him fight once. He had a chance to take the belt, in her opinion. That was two years ago, and she never knew what happened to him. Until now, anyway.

The door opened and the cart went through, stopping just beyond so Pussy could lock the door. The stairs waited in front of her, and she was tempted to take the cart that direction, but the sound of the elevator reaching the floor changed her mind.

It was a quick ride down, but the reaction as she exited was long on drama. Ignoring the gasps and murmurs, Pussy pushed the cart to the desk. Out of the corner of her eye, she saw two men in uniform rushing to meet her.

"Miss Katnip!" Olive's eyes bulged. "What happened? You're bleeding? Is he…." The words trailed off and she looked at him closely. "Who is that man? Why is he wearing one of our uniforms?"

"Funny, I was going to ask you that same question." Pussy held out a hand. "Do you have a napkin or kerchief I could borrow? I forgot to grab one before I left the room."

Olive pulled back and scanned beneath the desk before quickly grabbing a cloth and handing it over the desk. As Pussy brought it up to her lip the two uniformed guards arrived.

"I have no idea who he is. He attacked me in my room—after bringing in my luggage." Pussy pulled the cloth away. "You might want to look for the bellhop who was supposed to bring it to me."

"Good golly, Miss Katnip! I want to apologize on behalf of the hotel!" Olive motioned. There was a squeak in the wheel as the guards rushed the cart away from the sight of any other guests. "We'll comp you half your stay. And I promise to find out what that man was doing!"

"Olive," Pussy purred, "don't worry. It wasn't the hotel's fault. Just make sure that man spends a night or two in jail, if you don't mind. I don't want him coming back."

"He will never set foot on the premises again!" Pussy could almost hear Olive stomp her foot.

"Thanks, Olive." She turned and walked to the elevator once again. It was easy to ignore the looks she got. Her mind was very focused.

The numbers on the elevator panel beckoned her, and she responded. Number eight. The elevator lurched to a stop and she stepped clear. The sign indicated room 811 was on the left. A few seconds later she paused, ran her palms over her the front of her dress and her fingers through her hair, and then knocked.

As the door opened, the man beyond was already speaking. "It's about time! I was beginning to think that dame might have—" The words came to a dead halt as he saw her.

"Hi, Bulldog. I saw that you were staying at the same hotel, so I thought I might drop by and say hello." Pussy tried to keep an even expression as she spoke.

"P-P-P-Pussy!" He stepped back. "What are you doing here?"

"I just told you. There was some horse gossip that Bulldog Baxter was staying here, and I thought that was such a funny coincidence." She put her palm up on the door sill. "You think that's funny, don't you?"

"Yeah. Yeah, sure. A real laugher." She followed his eyes past her, desperation glazing them. "What, uh, what brings you to Big City?"

"Just looking for a friend. Do you know anything about that, Bulldog?" Pussy leaned in a little closer.

"What? No. No, I, uh, I don't know nothin' about no friend of yours." His head shook like it was trying to free itself from his neck. "I have no idea where she's at!"

"Where who's at?" Pussy pulled her hand down and crossed her arms.

"Uh, whoever it is you're lookin' for." She saw a small bead of sweat run down his temple.

"I never said it was a she, though, Bulldog. How'd you know that?"

"Lucky guess! Hey, look, I gotta go. I'm expecting a friend any minute now…yeah." Bulldog grabbed the door and began to swing it closed. Pussy stopped it halfway there.

"I hope you don't mean 'Ironhoof' Trotter," Pussy said. "I think he hurt himself. I saw him in the lobby. He looked like someone had beaten the tar out of him."

Bulldog's lips moved, but he never said anything.

"Hey, Bulldog, do you remember the last time we saw each other? You had that place next door when my club suddenly started having an odd infestation of pests. Then we had that misunderstanding when you accidentally entered my place when the exterminators were working." She moved her head slightly. "Does it still hurt when you turn your head to the left?"

"I…I…need to…to…" he stammered.

"Yeah, you need to go check on your friend." Pussy took a step back. "I want you to go see him, Bulldog. Maybe after that, you and I can have a talk or something. How's that sound?"

Pussy turned and took a step, but just one. "Oh, and Bulldog?" Her eyes became slits. "If I find out you've done anything to Jenny, you won't be able to run far enough away, got it?"

This time she walked on, taking her time to make every step count. When she heard the door slam behind her, her gait changed, moving a little more quickly to the elevator and then her room.

Brett Brooks

Chapter Six

The door closed behind her. Without taking another step, she stopped and closed her eyes. In a long, slow breath, she took in the mixture of smoke, grease, and alcohol. Her mouth slowly came open so that she could taste the aroma of the Kit Kat Klub on her tongue.

It was a thick, coarse, somewhat disgusting sensation, and she loved every moment of it.

"Foxy! Hi-de-ho, Honey."

She opened her eyes, and turned towards the voice. Foxy took slow steps towards the young woman who called to her, letting her eyelids close halfway. The faint sound of her lips smacking reached her own ears, but all anyone else might notice was her tongue teasing along the inside of her top lip.

By the time Foxy got to the hat check station, every inch of her body had been observed by the young lady behind the desk.

"You're here early." Foxy's fingers trailed along the edge of the counter separating the pair.

"I…I couldn't sleep." Robin fidgeted.

"Why not? I would have thought you were exhausted," Foxy said.

"I, uh, well, I was just so…." Robin ended the sentence with a giggle.

"I'm flattered." Foxy slowly closed her eyes and opened them again.

"You know I never…I mean, I wouldn't have thought that…." She giggled again. Foxy noticed her playing with the ends of her hair.

"Don't think about it. Just be happy." Foxy reciprocated, brushing back the hair off her face for just a moment. "You are happy, aren't you?"

"Cloud nine!" Robin almost answered before the question was finished, and she rose up on her toes, leaning into the counter from her side.

"Well, what's the problem, then?" Foxy took a step back. Robin did her best to take a step towards her, but the desk prevented it.

"There isn't one, I just…." Robin's voice trailed off and she lowered her head.

"Just what, Sweetie?" Foxy asked.

"I was wondering…what you…were doing tonight?" Robin seemed to turn a little more red, and Foxy pushed back a smile.

"Sweetie, with Miss Katnip out of town, I have to work the whole night. I'll be here all the way to closing and past that." She stepped back up to the desk. Foxy's hand came up and lay gingerly on the side of the Robin's scarlet face. The feathers ruffled up reflexively under her touch. "I'm not going to be able to do anything tonight."

"Oh. Oh, I…I see. I get it. It was a corny idea, I suppose."

Foxy felt her pulling away, and quickly wrapped her hand behind Robin's neck, holding her in place. Gently, she pulled her towards her. Their lips met, just for a moment, and Foxy tasted a hint of mint. Foxy let her grip fall free. When they pulled back, Robin stared at her with a blank expression.

"No," Foxy whispered. "It was a wonderful idea. It just can't happen tonight."

"Oh." Robin's mouth hung open. "I…maybe tomorrow?"

"We'll see, Sweetie." Foxy took a step back and turned her back to the other woman. She stood still, giving Robin a minute to take in the new view. Finally, she glanced back over her shoulder. "I promise though, it'll be soon."

She walked away, not waiting for a reply. In her mind, she saw Robin staring at her, lost for words until it was too late to say anything.

Foxy descended the short set of stairs at the end of the passage like liquid, flowing down from one to the next easily and softly, letting herself sway with every step. From the corner of her eye she saw Robby behind the bar, staring at her. It was easy enough to keep her eyes forward and pretend to not notice as she made her way towards the band.

Benji, the band leader and drummer, stood as she got closer. She stood a little taller than him, but his height didn't alter her view of him.

"Thanks for meeting me, Sweetie." Foxy stopped a few steps shy of him. "I know that you boys have a busy schedule."

"Happy to help out, Foxy," Benji answered. "What's the buzz?"

"I was hoping to talk you into changing up the set." Foxy pulled a set of papers from her dress. "I have a couple of ideas."

Benji's eyes narrowed. "Miss Katnip set up the whole set for the week before she left."

"Oh, I know, but," Foxy turned away enough that her face was barely in his view, "well, I just don't know if I would have the courage to do this when Miss Katnip was here. She's so good that…I just don't compare. I thought that maybe if I were to try something of my own I might gain enough confidence to try it when she came back." She turned to look back at him. "If you don't think that it's a good idea, though…."

"I never said that!" Benji brought his hand up, touching her on the arm. "And don't be so tough on yourself, Foxy. You're killer-diller, darling! I'd say right there with Miss Katnip."

"Oh, you're just being nice." Foxy laid her hand on top of Benji's, taking a moment to let her fingers trace up his lightly.

"No. No, I ain't. Foxy, you've got it. I've been around the biz for a bit. I started out playin' the skins for Cal Thompson over in Metroville. I've seen them come and go, and…." She saw his neck bulge as he swallowed. "I don't want to see you go, Foxy."

"Oh, Benji." Her hand moved up his arm to his face. His fur bristled slightly under her touch. "Sweetie, I'm not going anywhere. Not when I have the support of someone like you." With more motion than needed, Foxy looked around the room. Before Benji knew what was happening, she rose up on her toes and kissed him on the cheek.

She fell back flat to her feet and looked to the ground. "I hope you don't think I'm being forward, but…."

"N-no!" Benji stammered. "No, I don't think anything like that. That was, uh, nice. Real nice."

"I know it's probably wrong," Foxy added a little extra breath to her voice, "but I spend all night on the stage feeling ashamed and talentless. I think I only succeed because of you and your band. Is that wrong of me, Benji?"

Benji shook his head. "You ain't gotta worry about it. You ain't gotta worry about nothin'. Me and the boys, we got your back."

"That's so nice, Sweetie. I just hope…well, don't make a big deal out of it or anything. I don't want anyone to think that we're in cahoots somehow."

"Hey, it's on the down low. Ain't nobody here got to know nothin' about it." He took Foxy's hand in his, and she squeezed down in response. They stayed that way for a matter of seconds before he said anything else. "So, Foxy, you, uh, you busy after the show tonight? I could take you around. Introduce you to some of the other cats playing around town. I know Chief Bray, even. I bet he'd love to meet a dame with your kinda talent."

"Oh, Sweetie, I can't," she sighed. "With Miss Katnip out of town, I've promised to help Robby out with everything after close. Combine that with having to do a couple of extra shows tonight, well, I'm afraid I just won't have the stamina to hold up."

"Hey, I hear ya." She heard his voice turn softer. "Maybe tomorrow?"

"We'll see, Sweetie. We'll see." She stood taller, pulling herself back slightly. "But, tonight, you think you might be able to get the boys to do one of these numbers here?" Foxy handed him the music sheets. "Just one, maybe? Or more, if you're feeling it."

"I'm sure we can squeeze in one. You gonna be okay without practice?" Benji asked.

"Oh, I've been practicing, Sweetie. I think I can handle what you boys lay down." In a very deliberate motion, Foxy blinked. "But I gotta go help Robby now. You gonna be okay by yourself?"

"Don't you worry, Foxy." She heard him smack the music sheets against his thigh. "I won't let you down."

"Oh, you're the best!" She scrunched up her nose playfully. "I'll see you around."

"Yeah. See you," Benji answered.

She took one step back and then turned around, sashaying towards the bar. Her tongue ran over the sharp fangs in her mouth, feeling them almost bite into the soft flesh.

"Heya, Foxy!" Robby said as she got close. "You're in awful early."

"Hi, Robby." She pulled up onto a stool, laying her hands on the bar. "Well, with Miss Katnip out of town, I just want to make sure that everything goes perfect tonight."

"Hey, hey! Don't you worry. I've run the place for Miss Katnip before. It'll go silky." Robby popped a bar straw into his mouth, quickly positioning it to the corner.

"Oh, I have no doubt about you, Robby!" Foxy rubbed her fingers along the bar top, trailing them in small circles. "It's me I'm not sure about."

"You? You kidding, cousin?" Robby almost laughed. "I've seen you have the audience eating out of your hand. You ain't got a thing to worry about."

Foxy forced herself to frown. "I wish I had your confidence. Up to this point, I've had Miss Katnip there to keep me up. Every time that I've had a doubt or fear, she's been there to pick me up and keep me on my feet. And tonight…."

"And tonight you're going to do just fine!" Robby's hands moved below the bar, reappearing a moment later with a glass and a bottle. "Here. Take a shot. It'll calm you down."

Foxy watched him pour a finger of whiskey into the glass. He pushed it towards her, to the point where it brushed up against her hand. The glass felt cold against her touch. "I'm not sure, Robby. I'm afraid that it might have a bad effect on me."

"It's just one drink. And we still have a couple hours before we open, anyway. You'll be fine." He set the bottle down on the bar with a soft thump.

"You're right. I know you're right." Her mouth went open wide in a yawn, and she pulled her hand up to cover it. "Oh! I'm so sorry."

"Tired?" Robby asked.

Foxy nodded. "I'm afraid that I didn't get much sleep last night. I was up worrying about how well I'd do without Miss Katnip. I'm actually exhausted."

"You gonna be okay to sing?"

"Oh, I should be fine. I just—" Once again her mouth opened, and she tried to hide it with her hand. "Oh my! I'm so sorry. I guess I'm a little worse off than I thought." She looked up at Robby. "Hey, doesn't Miss Katnip stay here? Wouldn't that mean she has a bed upstairs?"

"Sure does," Robby began slowly, but his words picked up momentum quickly, "and I bet she'd be the first to insist that you go up there and take a nap before the show."

"Oh, Sweetie, do you think so? Are you sure she wouldn't be mad?" Foxy sped up her voice a little. "I sure could use the rest, and I think it'd be so much easier to sleep here."

"I know she wouldn't be mad. In fact, I'm in charge right now, and I insist that you go up those stairs and get yourself a good hour's nap!" He pulled the straw from his mouth and pointed to the second floor. "So, get up there!"

"Oh, Sweetie," Foxy purred, "you have no idea what this means to me. No idea."

"Hey, glad to help out."

Foxy grabbed the glass off the bar and downed the contents in one swallow. Before she pulled the glass away from her mouth, her tongue came out and licked around the inside of it. She set it down and looked back at Robby. His eyes were so wide it looked like he had no eyelids at all. "To help me sleep."

"Uh, yeah, well, no arguments from me," Robby replied softly.

"Robby," Foxy let his name roll out slowly, "I was wondering if, well, if you might be free tonight after we close down?"

He blinked. "Uh, yeah. Yeah, sure. No plans."

"Well, you've been so kind, I was wondering if maybe you'd like to stay a little late and maybe have a drink with me?"

"Uh, sure. Yeah. That sounds nice, actually." She watched him shift his weight from foot to foot.

"Great." Foxy stood up. "Oh, and do me a favor and keep it quiet. There's no reason to let anyone on the staff know that we're having a little time just for ourselves, is there?"

"Oh! Yeah. I mean, no. I mean, sure. You bet. I'll keep it mum, ma'am!" Robby quipped.

"Thanks, Sweetie." Foxy tossed her head, revealing for a split second the eye that seemed always hidden behind a sweep of hair. "I'll see you before we open, I promise."

He broke into a whistle, which gradually faded as she walked away. When her foot touched the bottom stair his whistle was little more than a whisper on the wind. Every step she took, sounds faded away, becoming less and less, replaced by the sound of her own heart pounding. She felt her mouth go dry and swallowed back, hoping to reclaim some moisture.

At the top of the stairs she took a moment to look back. She half expected to find them all staring up at her, and was slightly disappointed when they weren't. It was a short walk across the landing, and when she brought her hand to the doorknob she felt her fingers tingle, like a thousand pinpricks of lightning. Still, she gripped it and turned.

The room beyond was dark, lit only by a soft glow coming through the windows from the street. It took a moment for her eyes to adjust, but gradually shapes came into view. Enough to let her walk inside safely.

The door clicked shut behind her, and she deftly turned the lock above it. Her lungs slowly filled. The taste of club was gone, replaced by something sweet. Flowers with a hint of spice behind them. Her lip began to quiver, revealing a hint of fang in her mouth. Her mouth opened wide, and she pulled in as much as she could manage, letting the taste of the moment savor on her tongue. Slowly, her mouth closed and she pulled her lips tight, stretching them back into a long, thin smile.

"Finally," she growled.

Chapter Seven

Day and night have more than one difference. Shadows and light play distinct games at night, creating objects from the imagination, adding mystery to what you perceive. Daylight banishes those shadows, leaving behind what everyone thinks of as reality, and pushing created visions to the back of the mind.

Pussy thought the building before her would be, at the very least, uncomfortable at night. The worn facade and limited lighting—most of it coming from the neon on the building itself—combined with its location in a particularly unpleasant part of town would make the creative side of the brain happy to flex itself and impose something new.

As it was, the fading daylight only made the reality of the building rather clear. It also allowed her to do a complete head count of the unsavories lingering outside. One big one at the door, and four others moving up and along the street, drawing as much attention as possible. She'd seen this type before.

From the time Pussy left him last night, it took Bulldog almost twenty-four hours to make his move. During that time she waited patiently at the top of the long staircase, sitting in a chair she dragged from her room. At least the time gave her time to recover completely from the fight with Ironhoof. It took less than a half-hour for her lip to heal up, but another two before she felt her head clear completely. Still, she went back to her potion thrice more. Twice just to stay awake, and again right as Bulldog went down the elevator to the lobby. She wasn't too worried about him getting out before she got down there. An earlier conversation with her bellhop buddy, Phillip, made sure that the cab was a little slow in pulling up out front. By the time he was driving away, she was in her own cab, requesting that Bulldog's cab be followed at a safe distance.

Which led to here. The sign above the door read "The Butterfly Cage." She had a pretty good idea what kind of butterflies it held. She also was starting to think that Bulldog might be inside longer than she wanted.

"No offense, ma'am," the driver, a hog-like man, interrupted her thoughts, "but how long do you plan on staying here?"

Pussy reached into her clutch and pulled out a roll of bills. Her thumb rifled off a few sheets of green, and then handed them over the seat. "How long will this keep you here?"

He took the money and she watched him count it not once, but twice. "Lady, I'm here until sometime this weekend if you want."

"Just until I get back, if you don't mind. There is a chance I'll be in a hurry to leave when I return." Pussy pulled out a compact and opened it, turning her head left and right in an attempt to get a full view of her face.

"Uh, not to say anything bad, but, well, you do know what kind of place you've been staring at, don'tcha?" he asked quietly.

"Very." She snapped the lid closed and smiled politely. "Thank you, though. I appreciate your concern."

"Just be careful," he said. "I hear that place has some nasty folk who run it."

"I hope so." She opened the door. "Just have the car running when you see me, understand?"

"I'll be right here, ma'am," he confirmed.

Leaving the cab behind, Pussy walked across and down the street, garnering the attention of the men outside The Butterfly Cage well before she neared the front door. Two of them stood still as she passed, tempting her to turn back to make sure they stayed put, but she kept her eyes on her final destination— which was currently blocked by a rather large obstacle.

"Pardon me, but I'd like to pass." Pussy stayed a couple of steps off of him, hoping he would move aside. Considering the bulk of the bull-like man, she truly hoped that was all it would take.

She felt his eyes wander all the way up her body, from her toes to her face, lingering in some locations more than others. Behind her, she heard two others move close, but she made a point not to turn her head.

"Sorry, but no dames are allowed inside without a man with 'em. Management don't want no working girls inside the place." His lip curled up, revealing a gold tooth amidst all the yellowed ones. "At least none that ain't on the list."

"Well, then it's a good thing that I'm not in that line of work." Pussy kept her voice calm, completely hiding the emotion running through her.

"Uh-huh, right. Sorry, but you ain't getting in without a man, Chippy," he laughed.

She took a half step closer to him. "Check your list again. I'm sure that I'm on there somewhere."

He didn't even move. "You ain't on the list, lady. Sorry."

Her hand came out, moving toward the clipboard at his side. Grasping onto his wrist, she pulled it up slowly, feeling him provide growing resistance. She saw his face grimace slightly as he lost the battle to move the clipboard up between them.

"Check again." Her other hand came out and tapped on the clipboard, leaving something behind. "I'm right there, aren't I?"

As she let go, she felt his hand pull back, but only barely. His attention was focused exactly where she wanted.

"Yeah. Yeah, I see you there now, Miss." From her vantage, she was able to see him palm the cash she left on the clipboard. "I apologize for the confusion."

"Thanks. I appreciate you seeing things my way," Pussy said.

He rubbed his wrist where she had been holding it. Without waiting for him to open the door, Pussy moved past him and entered the building.

It took a moment for her eyes to adjust, but her lungs and ears didn't have that luxury. Repressing a cough, Pussy stepped into the smoke-filled chamber, trying to sort out the din encompassing her. A minute later she was able to truly take in her surroundings.

In the three seconds she allowed herself, she counted sixteen tables. Estimating ten people at each table, along with staff, those at the bar, and a few people just wandering about, there was likely two-hundred people here. Thankfully, only a handful paid her any attention as she entered.

Stepping further into the place, she melded with the group. Her eyes scanned over the tables again, hoping to see Bulldog at one of them. She couldn't be that lucky, of course. He was here. She knew it. She could almost smell him, even over the melange of cheap perfume and cigarettes. Stench like his was hard to hide.

Each table was packed, whether it be blackjack, craps, or roulette. Men trying to win money, and women trying to win men. Half the everyone who came here would be leaving with someone other than the one they started the night with—if they made it out at all. The number of goons around the perimeter was impressive. Whoever was in charge of this place took no chances.

Then she saw the doors. Twin slabs of wood with four men standing guard, each of whom would have to stoop to make it through the opening they protected. Pussy thought the doors were open just enough to give a glimpse of what lay beyond, if she could get close enough to see that far.

Only one way to find out. She walked straight towards the doors.

"Good evening, gentlemen." She spoke first. "I was wondering if you might be able to help me out."

"What is it you need, miss?" A narrow-eyed bull in an ill-fitting suit stepped forward.

"I heard that a friend of mine was here, and, well, I'm having trouble finding her. Do you know if she made it into that room there?" Pussy pointed past him.

"I'm sorry, miss, but I can't say. That room is private. Nobody is allowed to get into it without the, uh, management saying it was okay." He was doing his best to stay polite, but his awkwardness was showing.

Pussy took a small step to her left, angling to see through the doors. "Well, maybe you could get a message to her. Her name is Jenny. Jenny Foal."

"Miss Foal?" The big man stood up. "Yeah, she should be out in a bit. She's got a set in about ten minutes, I think. You want me to tell her you're here?"

"No. No, that's fine. I don't want to throw things off for her. I'll just wait for her to be done and then talk to her. Let her know that I'm here personally. I'm sure she'll be surprised to see me." She stared through the gap in the doors. The room beyond seemed large, maybe as big as the one they were in right now, but much darker and nowhere near as crowded.

"Well, then feel free to have fun at the tables until then." His hand moved to Pussy's shoulder, suggesting that she turn around and head back into the main room.

She decided to take the advice. "Thank you. You're very kind. I'll remember that."

As she stepped away, she looked over the room once more. There was no stage that she could see, nor a place for a band. If Jenny was going to perform, Pussy wasn't sure where it was going to happen.

The room offered plenty of vices, but Pussy passed them all by and made her way to the bar. Not only to avoid a potential waste of her time and money, but also for the vantage that it provided her. Not a perfect view, but certainly the best that the place had to offer. If you could even call it a view at all. Every time she looked around, Pussy found less and less that she wanted to see.

The swell of music seemed to come from nowhere, but the poor quality of it suggested second rate musicians who didn't want to show their faces. And then Pussy heard Jenny's voice, clear and unmistakable. A few seconds later she stepped into view, walking through the room and singing almost table to table.

Pussy sat back and watched. Jenny's voice was as strong as ever, but the way she moved was stiff and uneasy, and bags that could double as a matched set of luggage hung under each eye.

The moment Jenny saw Pussy her song faltered. A note sung off key. Just enough to confirm to Pussy what she thought. Pussy's reaction was simply to turn back around and motion the bartender over, ordering a dry martini she had no intention to drink.

Her hand rested on the glass for two more songs. Occasionally she picked up the glass and swirled its contents before putting back in place. When the music died down she pulled the glass closer to her, waiting.

"Hey, Joe. Can I get a seltzer?"

Pussy recognized the voice, but didn't turn her head. "I'm surprised to see you here, Jenny. This is nothing like Tinsel Town."

"Miss Katnip," Jenny whispered, "you've got to go. Get out of here, please."

"I thought you might be happy to see me. What's wrong, Jenny? What are you doing here?" Pussy picked up the glass and moved it in front of her face.

"I…I can't talk. I don't have time. Just, please, go back home. Go…." She hesitated. Pussy didn't let it hang clean.

"Talk to me, Jenny. I can't help you if you don't tell me what's wrong." Pussy's words were strong, but soft.

"I can't. My…. You gotta go, Miss Katnip. Don't worry about me. I'm fine. I just don't want anyone—"

Pussy cut her short. "You said 'my.' Your what, Jenny? What is it?"

The bartender set down the seltzer and Jenny picked it up, drinking down half of it in a moment. "Find my sister, Miss Katnip. Her name's Jill. Back in Mutt Town. Find her. Make her safe." Once more amateur music filled the room. "I gotta go."

Before she could take a step, Pussy grabbed Jenny's arm. "Do you need to leave?"

Jenny shook her head quickly. "I gotta work. I gotta, you understand?"

Pussy let her arm go. "I'll find her, Jenny. I'll find her and then I'll be back."

Without another word Jenny moved back into the room, her voice rising up as she disappeared from Pussy's view.

She waited for half of the song before Pussy stood up and walked away from the bar. Jenny's voice wafted through the room, like a ghost lost in the halls of an ancient castle, drifting away as Pussy moved to the exit.

Reaching the door she paused and turned back. At the far side of the room the twin doors she saw earlier opened and Bulldog stepped through them, flanked on either side by two men Pussy had never seen before. One of them, a wolfish man in a grey suit, looked directly at her, and it was obvious that he knew exactly who she was.

A finger shot up, and every eye around him looked her way. She didn't wait any longer, and exited the club.

"No business inside?" The bullish doorman laughed as she stepped outside.

"Plenty," Pussy answered. "Just not what I was hoping to find. I'll be back, though."

"Well, you might want to bring a man next time, doll. I don't know if the same trick'll get you in next time."

"Actually, I think I might just do that," Pussy answered. "See you another time."

With a purpose she strode down the street. By the time she started to cross the road a commotion rose behind her. She didn't turn around.

The taxi was right where she left it, and the driver started the engine before she got to it. By the look in his eyes, Pussy guessed that several others were coming up behind her rather quickly. She opened the door and sat down in the back seat.

"Drive," she said.

He didn't say a word, but threw the car into gear and hit the gas. A few fists bounced off the fenders as they pulled away, and Pussy took a second to glance out the window.

The man who pointed her out stood on the other side of the road. She took a second to memorize his face as the car sped down the street.

Brett Brooks

Chapter Eight

The train ride back to Mutt Town was uneventful, but far from relaxing. There was no one who came to the hotel to…visit her, thankfully, but Pussy didn't dare wait for that inevitability. Too many innocents were there, and Bulldog knew where she was staying. After she got back to the Fountain Royale she gathered her things and checked out immediately.

There was something deep inside that kept fighting her. Telling her that she wanted to go to another hotel. Stay in Big City and get Jenny out of that hellhole, one way or another. Then her mind wrapped around the problem. Specifically the "one way or another" part. The last thing that Jenny told her was to go back to Mutt Town and save her sister. Remove the threat controlling Jenny, and freeing her would become that much easier. It might not have been what she wanted to do, but it certainly was the smart thing to do.

Plus, there was that one other problem.

In the hours that she waited at the station for the noon train, Pussy swirled the bottle in front of her countless times. There was barely enough to even register. One dose. That's all she had left. No way that she could handle all those goons with just one dose. She needed to get back to the club. To her supply.

It was a long trip. And every time anyone walked past her, Pussy felt her hands tighten and her legs tense. They all kept on walking. It made her relax just a little—until the next one strolled by, anyway. Then it all started over again.

Finally back in Mutt Town, everything eased up. Slightly, at least. Tomorrow morning she would have to start looking for Jenny's sister—whoever that was. Jill. That's all the information she had. So, she would have to do a little research first. Shouldn't be too hard. Plenty of people at the club knew her well enough to get a description. There was a lot to do, but she would start with that.

After she had a long bath. That came first.

Pussy laughed at herself, and she saw from the corner of her eye the cabbie looking back at her in the mirror. All of this retrospection and concern displaced by the idea of warm water and soap bubbles. Her hand touched the ends of her hair, noticing the slightly greasy, frayed ends. The thought of taking time out to go to the stylist ran through her head, which rapidly morphed to the idea of taking a whole day to be pampered and preened.

A shake of the head cleared the thoughts away. Sticking with the bath would have to do for now. Once Jenny was back safe, then she could take the time for herself.

"We're here." The cabbie's voice broke her thoughts.

She looked out the window at the dark building. It was still early, but the sun was going down and the club was scheduled to open almost two hours ago. Opening the cab door and stepping onto the street, her eyes stayed on the club the whole time. By memory her hand slipped into her clutch and pulled out some money. She glanced down just long enough to make sure she had the right bill to hand over to the driver.

"Would you unload my bags, please?" she asked.

"Yes, ma'am!" The enthusiasm of his voice carried over to his quick step towards the trunk.

"Thank you. I'll have someone come out and gather them up in a minute, if you'd be kind enough to wait." Pussy glanced over at him and pulled another bill from her clutch. She held it towards him between fore and index fingers.

"Gladly." He took the bill like a lamb trying food for the first time. "I'll wait right here with them."

"It'll just be a moment." Pussy walked up the stairs to the front door. It didn't budge. She stopped awkwardly, almost walking into it directly. Without even realizing, she tried the door again, with no change in result.

The key went from her clutch to the lock in less than a second.

"Robin? Robert?" She called out their names before the door shut behind her. The lack of light in the room gave her the answer she didn't want. Intimate knowledge mixed with excellent vision and she walked straight to the main room of the club. Nothing. No one. Only a faint light from the kitchen shining through the doors.

Her head swiveled about as she trekked to the door, then she pushed it open and took a single step inside, holding the doors. The only thing in the room was the one fixture glowing like a spotlight staring at her from the ceiling. The doors finally swung closed after she turned and left.

The stairs waited. She answered with a slow, steady walk up to her office and apartment. That door opened easily, and she walked inside. More darkness.

A few steps brought her to the lamp beside the sofa. One more second brought it to life. Three more seconds passed before anything happened.

"Hello, Pussy."

She turned to the voice. Familiar, but not the same that she knew. It came from the edge of a razor now. "Foxy? What are you doing up here? What's going on? Where is everyone?"

Foxy was sitting in a high wingback chair. Pussy knew that it was blue, but in the dim light it took on a much darker tone. Her legs were crossed, with the top one swinging back and forth slowly. "That's a lot of questions. How about I answer them all at once: I sent everyone home."

Pussy narrowed her eyes. "You sent them home? And just how did you do that?"

"They didn't have a choice," Foxy pulled papers from the table beside her, "since I own this place now."

"I beg your pardon?" Each word Pussy spoke was clear and distinctive.

"Oh, don't you recognize this? This is the deed to the Kit Kat Klub. It's been signed over to me, by you." Pussy felt her hands clenching as Foxy flipped through to the last page, showing a set of signatures.

"I'm going to ignore the obvious forgery for a moment. How the hell did you get ahold of that deed?" Pussy growled.

"I'm so glad you asked!" Foxy jumped to her feet, and Pussy felt herself flinch forward, ready to meet her if necessary. It wasn't. Foxy turned and stepped behind the chair.

"I have to say, you're good. I knew that, of course, but still…. It took me almost an hour to find this." Far too casually for Pussy,

Foxy moved her hand over the wall, depressing the hidden button that opened the secret panel hiding her safe. "And this," Foxy gestured to the steel safe, "they just don't make them like this anymore. Cary and Co. out of Buffalo. One of the last models they ever made, with a C-5 direct drive straight-tailpiece lock. When they sold it there was a guarantee about it being unbreakable." She leaned back against it and dropped her hand down. The door opened with a slight groan under her effort. "Shame they aren't in business anymore. You could get some money from them."

"Impressive." Pussy stepped behind the davenport, letting her hand drag along the back of it. "I'll add safecracker alongside forger to the report when the police take you away. Though I suppose I could just sum it up as a petty thief."

"Oh, is that how you see me?" Pussy could hear it in her voice. Tension. Building up and waiting for release. "Well, then let me show you what else I found."

Foxy's hand moved onto the shelf beside the safe, hidden from Pussy by the placement of the chair. It returned holding a crystal decanter. One filled with a distinctive red liquid.

"I thought it was going to be in the safe. To be honest, I was very shocked—and a little bit frustrated—to find that it wasn't. The deed was wonderful, but this…this is what I truly wanted." Foxy shook her head. "It took me a little while to figure out that you kept it hidden in plain sight. Just another bottle among the others at your own personal bar up here."

"What is it? Wine?" Pussy's hand gripped the back of the davenport.

"No, in fact it's not." Foxy swirled it around. "You know exactly what this is, and more importantly, so do I. I know so much about it."

Pussy allowed herself a smile. "Well, I doubt that's true." She stepped from around the davenport, standing some feet away from Foxy.

"What is it that you call it? Fizz?" Foxy shook her head. "Such a stupidly simple name for such an amazing creation."

"Who told you that?" Pussy inquired.

"Oh, Pussy," Foxy laughed. "Don't worry. I'm not in cahoots with anyone here."

"I never doubted them. I just wanted to know who you've been talking to." Pussy looked at the decanter. The level was noticeably lower than she left it.

"Everyone. No one. What's the difference?" Foxy sighed.

"You aren't the first person to come looking for that, you know. There have even been a couple of people who took a drink. They didn't care for the taste." The distance between them was only about ten feet. Pussy mentally measured it and the time needed to cover it.

"It is a little bitter," Foxy placed the bottle back down on the shelf, "but I kinda liked the taste."

"Shame it won't do you any good." Pussy set her feet. "That's an old family recipe, and it only works if your a part of my family. And I just don't see the family resemblance."

"Is that so?" Foxy purred.

It was almost faster than Pussy's eye could follow. Foxy turned around, putting both hands on either side of the three-foot-tall safe. It looked as though she simply twisted her body back, not adding any athletic motion at all. Pussy couldn't swear to it though, as all of her focus was on the safe flying directly towards her.

Only one option presented itself, so Pussy took it and leapt to her left. The safe crashed to the floor, miraculously not smashing through it, as Pussy rolled to her feet. She didn't hesitate to make her next move a sprint towards Foxy.

She slipped up past any defense, leading with her right fist, and drove it squarely into Foxy's jaw. Her fist stung from the blow, but at least Foxy's head jerked back from the impact, taking her up off her feet at the same time. Foxy fell to the ground with a heavy sound.

"How did you do that?" Pussy more demanded than ask. "That safe weighs close to half a ton. There's no way you should be able to lift it."

Foxy sat up. Pussy saw a darker spot of red fur around Foxy's mouth. "Half a ton? Really? Tell me, are you able to pick it up?"

Once more Foxy moved with dizzying speed. Foxy kicked herself up, and was on top of Pussy before she had a chance to move. She saw Foxy's right hand move sideways, but couldn't get out of the way before it contacted Pussy's face and turned her whole body. She chose to go with the momentum, and spun around to face Foxy, fist first.

Pussy's swing met empty air. Foxy's didn't.

The force of Foxy's blow sent Pussy flying backwards, crashing into the hallway. She brought her face up just in time to see Foxy reach down and firmly grip the top of her dress. Her whole body jerked as she was yanked upwards.

"You really have no idea how much I'm going to enjoy this," Foxy growled.

It was a good ten feet from where they stood to the twin doors of the apartment. Pussy went through them like they were a sheet of paper, tumbling head over heels until finally stopping against the railing surrounding the landing.

Pussy gathered herself quickly. Standing up proved to be a bit more difficult than she thought, as a sharp pain ran through her knee. It didn't matter. She readied herself as Foxy casually walked towards her.

Bracing with her good leg, Pussy kicked out, but her leg didn't come back down. Both of Foxy's hands grabbed onto Pussy's ankle, but only long enough for her to use it to toss Pussy off the balcony.

The table below her did it's best to break her fall, and Pussy did everything that was needed to shatter the table as she landed. Something else broke when she landed, too. Pussy felt a sharp pain in her side from cracked ribs.

Pussy staggered as she stood, just as Foxy landed beside the table. From where she landed, Pussy knew that she had to have jumped from the balcony, but it looked like she simply hopped down off a small step.

"Look at you," Foxy snarled. "You can barely stand."

The broken leg of the table was at Pussy's feet, and she wasn't going to ignore it. She wasn't going to be able to use it either. By the time her hand wrapped around the wood, Foxy had gotten ahold of her. Foxy slapped her hand from the table leg, grabbed the front of Pussy's dress, and lifted her into the air.

"I could kill you right now," Pussy knew she was right, "but I won't. I'm not done with you, yet. I want to take everything from you. Take everything that you hold dear. Just like everything was taken from me."

Pussy felt Foxy's hand slide up, gripping her around the throat, while still keeping her dangling in the air. "This is probably so confusing for you. How can this be? This is an ancient Katnip secret. It only works on your bloodline. Well, maybe you should talk to your mother about that. Oh, wait. She doesn't speak to you anymore, does she?"

Disorientation washed over Pussy as she was lifted higher into the air. Her body being smashed through a second table brought everything into a crystal clear world of pain.

"You know," Pussy could hear Foxy speak, but locating her was proving to be a challenge, "my original plan was to seduce you. Make you fall for me. And then, when everything was perfect, I was going to break your heart—and then move on to other parts of your body."

Something grabbed ahold of Pussy. It was Foxy, she was sure of it. It must have been. The ground began sliding against her back. Turning her head to the side, she saw the length of the bar passing by at ground level. The perspective made her think that maybe she should have the foot railing replaced. Why was she thinking about that right now? What was going on?

"Unfortunately, you proved to be a cold-hearted bitch." Foxy's voice again. It was coming from somewhere near her feet. Her foot was in the air, actually. Something—no, someone was holding it. "So, I had to let that go, but don't worry, I still found plenty of folks here at the club who were much warmer to my approach."

Pussy felt her head banging up and down in a steady rhythm. Steps. She was going up steps. And then she was flying again. Just long enough to find the end of the hallway. Her body slid down the wall, crumpling when she reached bottom. She saw a pair of high heels walking up towards her. Black. Polished.

The world spun for a second, and when it came to a stop, Pussy was staring into Foxy's face. A set of fangs poked out from beneath Foxy's lips.

"Understand this: Sometime soon I am going to come find you, but not until I have seen you reduced to nothing. You're going to be dreaming of this moment and wishing that things were this good again." Foxy leaned in and Pussy felt something soft against her lips, but just for a second. "And then...then I'm going to end you."

Cold air rushed over Pussy's back. "Now get the hell out of my club."

Suddenly, she was tumbling across the cement on the street outside. She hit something stacked on the sidewalk, sending it sprawling. It looked like luggage. Her luggage.

A figure came into view. A man. In a taxi uniform.

"Lady? Lady, are you okay? Lady? Aw, geez! Somebody call somebody!"

He was talking to her. Yelling. How? He was so far away. And he kept slipping farther and farther back, fading into the darkness that enveloped her.

And then he, and everything else, was gone.

Red is the Darkest Color

Brett Brooks

Chapter Nine

He liked it this way. The people, all of the people, coming into his club and spending their money. It was just like he always imagined it. And up to this point all he was able to do was imagine it. There were more people in his club tonight than he had ever seen before, and he was loving every second of it.

Boss Dogg pulled the cigar from his mouth and held it near his chest. The smoke rose up and circled his head, letting him take in the aroma as he stared out at the people spending money. His waitresses were running around like rabbits, and the band looked to him as though it was about to fall over from exhaustion.

His cigar went back into his mouth. The normal stale taste of the cigar was gone, replaced with something far more enticing. Something about this many people made everything seem a little more fresh. The sound of them talking, laughing, drinking, and just being nearby washed over him. Maybe with the money he was spending he'd be able to buy good cigars instead of the cheap thing he was smoking now.

"Hey Boss!"

He turned to see his prime enforcer. "Mugsy! How are you on this glorious night?"

"Uh…okay, I guess. What's so glorious about it?" Mugsy scratched the back of his head.

"This!" Boss gestured wide, taking in the gathering. "These people! Have you ever seen a crowd like this here?"

"Gosh, no! This place never even gets half this many people. Nobody likes this place."

For a moment Boss considered his response, but not tonight. Not on a night like this. "The Dogg House is a very popular club, Mugsy. And from the looks of things tonight, our reputation is spreading. We've got a full house, after all."

"Well, sure, but that's probably because the Kit Kat is closed," Mugsy stated.

"What?" He spun towards Mugsy. The giant oaf almost leapt back from him when he did. "What do you mean it's closed?"

"Yeah, there was a sign on the door. Says that the place is closed down until tomorrow, I think. Something about a new model or something." Mugsy stared up, as though he was hoping to see what he was trying to recall on the ceiling.

Boss snapped his fingers. Multiple times. It seemed to be enough to pull Mugsy back. "What did the sign say, Mugsy? What exactly?"

"Uh, I'm not sure. That was over an hour ago that I read it."

"An…hour ago?" Boss almost bit through his cigar. "You've known about this for an hour and you're just telling me about it now?"

"Should I have told you sooner?"

"Yes, Mugsy. Yes, you should have." Boss looked out over the crowd. They looked a little rambunctious. "Eh, let's move this to the office. I don't want to talk around the customers."

"Sure thing, Boss!" Mugsy moved in front, clearing the way. Boss knew that the big man's size was enough to clear most, but when needed, he wasn't shy about using his hands. A habit that was fine most of the time, but right now, with this crowd here spending money....

"Mugsy!" Boss stepped in front of the big man. "Just stay behind me."

"Uh, sure thing, Boss." He could feel Mugsy looming behind him. Maybe that was a good thing. It'd give him a little more presence. Make him seem bigger.

Just one step inside his office, Boss stopped cold. He had a visitor.

"Foxy?" She sat in his chair. Behind his desk. With her feet propped up on it. Her dress fell open over her thighs, revealing all of her long legs. He tried not to stare. At least not for too long. "What are you doing here?"

"Great crowd you've got tonight." Foxy's voice went up and down like a song.

"Yeah, it's decent." Boss stepped in and motioned behind him. He heard Mugsy shut the door. "But you didn't answer my question. Why you here? We ain't supposed to meet up for two more days."

"Well, I have a report, and I thought you might want to hear it now." Her feet came down off the desk and she leaned forward. "It's done."

"Done? What? What's done?" Boss asked.

"The Kit Kat Klub is under new management," she stood up, "and you're looking at her."

Boss let the words run through his head a couple of times. "Are you saying that…."

"Pussy is no longer in business." Foxy walked around in front of the desk. "Foxy is, though."

"That…that may be the best news I've ever heard!" He pushed his chest out and strutted over towards Foxy.

"I thought that part might make you happy." She leaned back as he approached, resting against his desk. For a brief moment, he was jealous of a piece of wood.

"Very happy! You did great, Foxy. Now all we have to do is decide what to do with it." Boss scratched his chin. "I suppose we could sell it, but that'd just be opening up new trouble."

"Oh, don't worry. It's going to stay open. I'll be running it personally," Foxy replied.

"That's a thought. You could run the joint, and we could split the profits fifty-fifty." Visions of new income moved through Boss's mind.

"Close. I'll be keeping all of that money. You'll be splitting the money you make from this garbage dump with me, sixty-forty."

Boss blinked. "I must've misheard you, Foxy. You meant to say that you wanted to keep sixty percent of the Kit Kat, right? We might be able to—"

"You heard me correctly." Foxy interrupted. "You're going to give me sixty-percent of what you make here. And you're going to thank me each time you do."

He moved the cigar in his mouth from one side to the other. "Foxy, doll, I appreciate all the help in getting rid of that Katnip broad, but don't get your skirt all up around your shoulders. You work for me, remember?"

"Actually, you've done everything that I wanted, not the other way around." Foxy stood there acting calm and easy, as though she was safe in this room. Boss decided it was time to correct that misconception.

"Foxy," he pulled the cigar out and used it to point at her, "at best we were helping each other. Now…." Boss shrugged and turned to his enforcer.

"Mugsy." Boss put the cigar back in his mouth and pointed twice at the woman behind him.

Boss saw a slight hesitation before Mugsy stepped past him. He turned to watch the events unfold.

"Foxy, I'm real sorry about this," Mugsy said, "but the boss said I gotta, so…. It's a real shame. You're a real dish."

Foxy stood there, still leaning back against Boss's desk, with just a slight smile on her face. Boss shook his head, sad to think that he'd probably never see that smile again. Then Mugsy reared back, and swung in a wide arc, putting all of his weight behind the punch.

Which made the fact that Foxy caught it in her own hand and stopped it cold that much more startling. Mugsy's right hand was clenched in Foxy's left and it wasn't moving. Not at all. Neither forward nor back.

"Mugsy!" Boss shouted. "Stop fooling around."

"I…I ain't." The strain of Mugsy's muscles became perfectly clear. "She…she just…."

"You have another hand, Mugsy!" Boss informed him.

He responded with his left fist lashing out. Somehow it never connected. It looked to Boss like Foxy simply leaned back away from it.

"Mugsy," Foxy said softly, "who is the boss here?"

"Well, Boss is the boss," he answered.

"Try again," she stated softly.

Something happened. Boss watched Mugsy fall to his knees suddenly. Mugsy's left hand reached up and grabbed ahold of Foxy's left hand, still wrapped around his right. It almost looked like he was trying to ask her to marry him.

"Who...is...boss?" Foxy spoke a little louder, and a little slower.

"M-Mugsy," Boss stammered, "get up! Get on your feet!"

"I...I can't, Boss. She...she's got me—"

Mugsy cut himself off, changing from words to a sharp scream. Foxy leaned in and he crumpled backwards. The only reason Mugsy didn't hit the ground was because she was holding him off the ground by his hand. Boss swore he heard the sound of something cracking.

"I'm going to ask this one more time, Mugsy. This is the last time. After that, I'm going to lose my temper." Her lips curled up and Boss saw her fangs. He took a large step backwards. "Who. Is. Boss?"

"Y-you are," Mugsy whimpered. "You're boss, Miss Foxy! You're boss!"

She let go of his hand, and Mugsy immediately pulled it tight against his body. Her other hand came around and gently patted the wolfish man on his cheek. "See? Was that so hard?"

Then Boss saw her look at him. When something bounced off of his chest he realized that his cigar had slipped free from his mouth.

She started walking towards him. If circumstances were different he would have noticed the wide sway of her hips and the curve of her legs. Instead, all Boss could see was her one visible eye. One pale grey eye, that somehow had a fire burning inside it.

He felt himself swallow reflexively when she stopped just shy of him.

"Now, Mr. Dogg, do you understand your position? Or do I need to explain things further?" The winter wind outside had nothing on Foxy's voice.

"No. No, B…Bo…Boss." He somehow forced the word out. "No, I got it."

"Good." With casual disregard, she turned her back to him and stood there. The back of her head was right in front of him. There was nothing she could do. He could easily just drive his fist into it. And for a brief moment he even balled his fist tight.

And then he looked past her and saw Mugsy, still kneeling, holding his right hand tenderly in his left. Boss relaxed his hand and watched Foxy walk back to his desk. She walked around and sat down in his chair. Then she pulled his cigar box over and took one out. With more spectacle than needed, Foxy bit off the end of one it and spit that tiny piece onto the floor. Her head turned slowly to look back at him.

Boss felt her eyes burrow into him. The collar of his shirt grew uncomfortably tight and he felt it soak damp with his own sweat.

"Is…is there something you need, Miss Foxy?" His voice cracked as he spoke.

"So kind of you to ask, Mr. Dogg." She pointed towards the door with the cigar. "I need you to go back out into the club and make sure all of our guests are happy. We want everyone to be happy now, don't we?"

"Sure thing, Miss Foxy," Boss answered quickly. "Sure thing."

As quick as possible he spun around and moved to the door. He didn't want to move too quickly, but he definitely wanted to get out of that room as fast as possible. As he was closing the door, he heard Foxy speak one more time.

"Mugsy," she purred, "why don't you come over here and… light my cigar."

The door clicked behind him and Boss could hear nothing but the din of the crowd, droning just below the level of the music playing. It sounded sour and off key.

He watched the people sitting together, laughing and doing their best to talk to each other over the rest of the crowd. Absentmindedly, he reached to his pocket to pull out a new cigar. All he found was an empty hole. He glanced over his shoulder, seeing the door to his—to her office. He wiped his fingers along the sleeve of his coat.

A bright and happy laughter briefly preceded someone bumping into him. He turned to see a cute little lamb of a girl staring up at him.

"Oh, sorry," she giggled. "Hey! You're the guy who owns this place, right? You've got a great club!"

He just stared down at her. She waited a moment and the turned and walked off, her laughter coming back as soon as she took her first step. His eyes followed her all the way to her table, where she was quickly pulled onto the lap of a wolfish man sitting there.

"All these people. What a bunch of chumps." He snorted. "I hate this place."

Boss Dogg walked towards the bar, raising two fingers towards the bartender halfway there.

Brett Brooks

Chapter Ten

Her eyes fluttered and light attacked her senses. As the world slowly came into focus she found herself in a completely unfamiliar setting. The bed was large, and soft enough, but the room lacked any real sense of style. Nothing hung on the walls, and the drapes covering the windows were best described as serviceable. She spied a table beside the bed, and a dresser rested on the wall across from the foot of the bed. A few things rested on the dresser, but she couldn't make out any details. It was slightly blurry. There were two doors, one completely closed and the other barely cracked open. The closed one she assumed led to a hallway, and the other likely a closet or bathroom.

Pussy sat up, and almost fell backwards from the effort. Pain shot through her head, but she was able to ignore it thanks to the more sharp, stabbing pain on her left side. Reflexively she grabbed her ribcage, wincing from the slight contact. Air sucked in through her teeth when she slowly turned in the bed, hanging her bare legs over the side.

It was at that point she realized that she was naked, and her clothes were nowhere to be seen. The pain in her leg as she stood up was almost enough to force her back down onto the bed, but she endured. She just wished whatever was causing that high-pitched whine would go away. Limping to the dresser, she opened drawers until she found what she wanted. All of the clothes were meant for a man, but they would have to do. She tried on a pair of pants, but the waist was far too large and there was no belt available. The formal shirt she pulled out fit more like a dress, and she just let it hang down to mid thigh. Her tail pulled up the bottom of the shirt's back, almost bringing it too high, but she didn't care at this point.

She went to the slightly opened door. A bathroom. The closest thing to a smile that she could manage crossed her face as she stepped up to the sink. It quickly faded when she saw her reflection. The bruise around her left eye went almost a third of the way down her cheek. Very carefully she brought her fingers up to it, happy to discover that, despite its look, it wasn't overly sensitive like her ribs.

There was soap, and there was a towel, and she decided to put them to good use. The warm water felt like a welcome blanket on her face. Five minutes later, her brief birdbath had her back to almost feeling like herself.

"Pussy?"

She tensed at the sound of her own name, and instantly regretted it. Every part of her body hurt. A second later she registered the voice.

"George?" She poked her head out of the bathroom. He was standing in the other doorway with an expression bordering between panic and relief. When he turned to look at her, it shifted firmly to the latter.

"Oh, thank goodness." His whole body seemed to relax with those words. "I've been so worried."

"I…thank you," she answered. Too many questions ran through her mind. She went with the simplest one. "Where am I?"

"My apartment. Sorry about how it looks, I just, well, I don't get many visitors." He scratched himself behind the ear.

Pussy went ahead and stepped out of the bathroom. George's eyes drifted quickly down her whole body before he quickly turned his head away. His already reddish face turned almost crimson.

"How did I get here?" Pussy asked.

"Uh, well, that's actually kinda a long story. The short version is that I got a call about you being unconscious outside your club. I picked you up and brought you here." He turned his body slightly, and Pussy could tell it was to make it easier to not look her way.

"You got a call?" Her mind went back to the last thing she remembered. "I was…I was outside the Kit Kat. I was…." Everything came back. "Foxy."

"She called the cops, Pussy," he said. "Told them that you broke into the club and threatened her. That she had to defend herself against you."

The fur on the back of Pussy's neck went up. "Did she?"

"Yeah. A friend of mine on the force is the one who called me. I showed up to get you after she told them that she didn't want to press charges, she just wanted you out of there." George almost turned to look at her, but stopped himself just short. "Hey, uh, I'm sorry about the clothes. Your dress was ripped to shreds."

"So, you undressed me when you put me in bed?" she asked softly.

"No!" George answered so quickly that Pussy almost laughed. "No, I got Mrs. Drake from next door to come over and take care of that. I just came in to check on you. I never looked under the covers, I swear!"

"George," Pussy said gently, "don't you worry. I've never thought of you as anything but a perfect gentleman."

He paused. Pussy could tell that he wanted to say something, and she was pretty sure it wasn't what ended up coming out of his mouth. "Well, I don't have any clothes for you, and Mrs. Drake is way too big for her stuff to fit. I'm sorry."

"Do you have a belt?" she asked.

"Yeah, sure," he said.

"Get me one of those, and we'll go from there." She stepped over to the dresser and pulled out the pair of pants she found earlier. George pulled the belt from around his waist and held it out. She took a couple of tender steps and took it.

"Why…why don't you get dressed, and I'll go fix some coffee. I imagine you'll want to get something inside you," he said.

"I just might," Pussy purred. George stiffened up a bit. "Go ahead, George. I'll be out in a couple of minutes."

He nodded and stepped out of the room, pushing the door to as he left. Pussy moved back to the bed and sat down. It was very tempting to lay back down immediately. Instead, she rolled up the cuffs of the pants, and pulled them up. They hung very loosely off her, pulled tight at her waist by a belt moved to the last hole that barely held them up.

She stood up, ready for the pain this time, and ran her fingers through her hair, pulling it back behind her head. Twisting it around, she tied it up into a loose bun.

When she made it to the hallway, the smell of brewing coffee hit her like a brick. Her mouth was watering by the time she reached the kitchen.

"Oh God, George. That smells amazing."

He turned to her and froze. "Um, thanks. You…have a seat."

"I can be talked into that." The small kitchenette had seen better days, but the chair still had cushion on it, which felt like a throne to her at the moment.

George poured a pair of mugs, and put one in front of her before sitting down across the table. "So, are you able to tell me what really happened?"

Pussy took a sip of the coffee. He served it to her black. It was strong and bitter, and she didn't mind a bit. "What, you don't believe Foxy's story?"

"How many years have we known each other?" he replied.

She chuckled. "She duped me, George." Pussy took another sip of coffee. "And then some, actually."

"Duped you? So that's how you got all those bruises?" he countered.

"Yeah, well, she also hit me right in my overconfidence." Pussy leaned back in the chair, stretching out her back and rolling her shoulders. "And everywhere else, too, I think."

There was a pause before George spoke. "How?"

"What do you mean, how?"

"Just that. It's like I just said, Pussy. We've known each other for a long time. I've seen you beat the tar outta guys three times your size." His eyes narrowed. "How did that…how did Foxy do that to you?"

The look in his eyes was one that she had seen before. She just wasn't sure she was ready to give him what he wanted. The warmth of the coffee radiated through the ceramic mug and warmed her hand. She turned her head and saw dim sunlight outside.

"How long have I been here?" she asked.

"Almost a full day," he answered, "and you're avoiding the question."

"You're right, I am." She brought the coffee mug to her lips and took a long sip. When she put it back on the table he was still staring at her with that same look. A deep sigh came out. "All right."

Pussy stood up and walked towards the stove. The cold tile floor grew warmer as she got closer to the cabinets. She took a moment to refill her coffee mug and then shifted to lean back against the counter beside the cooktop.

"It's called Fizz." After another sip of coffee she set the mug down on the counter. "At least, that's what I've always called it."

"What is?" George asked.

"It's…well, I suppose you would call it a potion. I've always thought of it as a drink, but a drink doesn't do what it does." Memories flooded through her mind. "It's something that my mother taught me. And her mother taught her. The women of the Katnip family have handed it down, mother to daughter, for centuries."

"I don't understand. A potion? What kind of potion?" She heard George turn his chair to face her directly.

She took a deep breath. "What you've seen me do, it's because of something I call Fizz. I drink it and for a time I have increased speed, strength, durability, and I heal fast. I also get these...visions. My mind opens up and lets me see things that I normally might miss."

"Wait, you have a drink that gives you...super powers?" She heard more than just a slight tone of disbelief.

She hesitated. "I suppose you could call it that. To me it's just been a part of who I am."

"You...you're serious." She heard it that time for certain.

"I am, George." The previous night hit her. "Of course, not everything seems right anymore." She picked up her mug and moved back to the table, sitting across from George once more. "Like I said, my mother passed the legacy of Fizz down to me. Along with it she gave me the history of it."

Her fingers trailed along the rim of her mug. "According to the tale, about five-hundred years ago my ancestors were a part of a group of druids living in southern England. A tyrannical ruler by the name of Cedric the Bold, The Duke of Dragonshire, came to terrorize them and the other people under his rule. My ancestor developed the potion that I call Fizz, and used the abilities it gave her to fight back against him. She became a champion to the people. Ever since, the women of the Katnip line have done the same thing. Fight for those in need, against those who would do wrong."

"This...is...." George struggled to finish his thoughts.

Pussy finished for him. "Hard to believe? I know. It's one of the reasons I never tell anyone about it."

"It would explain a lot, though." It was George's turn to stand and walk to the counter. She let him have his space. After just a moment he turned back to her. "What it doesn't explain is how Foxy was able to…." He didn't finish his sentence.

"Beat the living hell out of me?" Pussy said it for him. "No, it doesn't. I was told—and had seen firsthand—that the potion only worked on my family line. Foxy isn't any family that I'm aware of, either. She even pretty much said that as a fact last night." She absent-mindedly rubbed her sore ribs. "There's no doubt that the Fizz worked on her though."

"Wait," George broke her chain of thought, "Foxy took your potion?"

"She did. And I have to say, it worked on her better than it works on me. She was stronger, faster, and a hell of a lot tougher." Pussy stared blankly ahead, not seeing the kitchen at all. "She really could have killed me last night."

"Kill you? Why?" George whispered loudly.

"I was sitting here wondering that same thing, actually. Up until she started working at the club, I'd never seen her before in my life. The way she was talking…." Pussy stood up. The pain was lessening each time. "George, did you bring any of my luggage?"

"Luggage? There was no luggage when I found you," he replied.

"Damn. She must have taken them." Pussy took a few steps out of the kitchen and into the living room. George followed. "It makes sense, I suppose. She said something about taking everything of mine and ruining me, or something like that. I was a little…woozy when she said it."

"Well," George stepped past her, and she didn't see what he walked to until he turned around, "you did have this."

He held out her clutch purse. She took it and opened it up. Somehow, it was still there.

The small crystal bottle with the red liquid inside rested in her hand.

"Is that what I think it is?" George asked.

"Yes, it is. And it's all I have left." Pussy put it back in the clutch, snapping the purse shut tightly. She held onto the purse, pulling it slightly closer to her body. "George," she looked him directly in the eye, "I'm going to have to leave."

"Not until you've healed up, you won't!" he said instantly.

It was a valiant response. Pussy appreciated that. "Actually, I need to leave tonight. Soon. Foxy is going to know that I came here, and she's going to come looking for me. I don't want to be here when either she or the people that she sends get here."

"I won't let them hurt you, Pussy." The sentiment behind his words carried a lot of weight.

"I won't let them hurt you, George. And the easiest way for that to happen is for me to not be here, and for you to tell them everything that you know. Cooperate completely." Pussy stepped up to him.

"That sounds ominous," he stated.

"No, it just means I'm not going to be able to tell you where I'm going, or why. You can't know what I'm doing. If you don't know, then you can't be accused of lying."

"I want to help you, Pussy," he pleaded.

Her hand came up and gently brushed his cheek. "I know you do. And that means so much to me," she pulled her hand back, "but you can't. I'm sorry."

For almost half a minute, they stood there. Pussy started to pull away, but a pair of hands grabbing her arms prevented it.

"Don't leave me, Pussy. I don't want that." The passion in George's voice was ten degrees above warm.

As gently as she could, Pussy pulled out of his grasp. "Then don't think of it as me leaving. I just have to go away for a bit, starting right now."

"Why? Why now?" George started to take a step towards her, but stopped himself.

Pussy did take a step away, heading to the front door. "Because, like I said, Foxy will be here shortly, and she's not going to be happy. You see, she didn't really get what she was looking for at the Kit Kat. And I'm guessing that she's figuring that out, right about now."

Pussy allowed herself a small smile.

Red is the Darkest Color

Brett Brooks

Chapter Eleven

"Where is it?" she screamed.

The table crashed into the wall, shattering to splinters and joining the rest of the broken furniture littering the room. Foxy kicked the debris, scattering it from her feet. Almost all of the furniture in the room was lying in shambles, as well as more than a few of the built-in shelves.

Joining the wood were other items in various degrees of destruction. Books torn in two. Vases shattered to glass fragments. A pair of silver candlesticks. Pillows. Sculpture. All of it cast off, seemingly as refuse. And beneath most of it was the torn remnants of luggage brought in off the street, and the contents of them scattered about like leaves cast to the wind.

The one section that looked untouched was the bar. Liquor and glasses, all lined up in a row, and all intact. Foxy walked towards it, kicking pieces aside as she moved, and running her fingers casually through her hair.

Turning over a glass, she first picked up a bottle of brown liquid. She pulled the stopper out and took a moment to wave it under her nose. With a slight nod of her head she turned the bottle up, pouring out about an inch of whiskey into the glass.

She brought the glass to her mouth and took a drink. The glass went back to the bar.

"I'll give you this, Pussy, you have good taste." Foxy picked up the bottle at the back of the bar. A crystal decanter filled with red liquid, and added a large splash of it to her whiskey. With a twist of her wrist she swirled the concoction together, turning the liquid to a very rich, dark reddish-brown. The glass came up again, and she downed the contents in a single shot.

She felt it building up inside her, starting deep. A jolt of electricity wanted to race through her, break free and shoot through her limbs, but she wouldn't let it. As tightly as a clenched fist, she held the power in check, letting it grow and build inside her. Every second pushed further and further, attempting to push her to the very edge of her limits.

And then her whole body shuddered, and the power found release. She felt it course through her, running from the core of her being to the tips of her fingers and the end of her toes. Her breath came out in a broken exhale, followed immediately by fast, shallow breaths.

Her tongue snaked out and pulled the last vestiges of the liquid from her lips. She held that small amount in her mouth, causing it to tingle from lips to throat.

"Foxy, I—" She turned to the door just as it opened. Robby was already talking as he stepped inside. His words came to as sudden a stop as his feet. "What kinda mess you got goin' on up here? Is everything okay, or did you snap your cap?"

"Oh, Robby," Foxy purred and slinked her way across the floor. She chose her steps carefully this time, avoiding everything in her path. "I'm glad you came up here. I was wanting to talk to you."

"Uh, sure." His eyes were scanning around the room, taking in the destruction. Foxy wanted them to be on her only.

"Robby," she said softly. And then a little more forcefully. "Robby!" He snapped his head around. "I need to know if Pussy had anyplace else here in the club. I'm looking for…I mean, she told me to find something for her, and, well, I can't. As you can see, I've almost torn this place apart looking for it, and I'm worried that I might not be able to get it and…and I'm just not sure what will happen to Pussy if I can't find it."

"Well, y'see Foxy," his hand went up behind his head and she saw him scratch the back of it, "I kinda wanted to talk to you about that. There's a bit of a scuttle going around the club that Miss Katnip came by here last night. Do you know anything about that?"

"Came by here?" Foxy feigned surprise. "That can't be right, Robby. I was here all night. I'm sure I would have at least seen her if she was here."

Robby shook his head. "I dunno, Foxy. Somethin' about this just don't seem right. I got a bad feeling about it." His eyes moved back to the room and the carnage around them. "And what is it you're lookin' for that made you do this?"

"It's paper. A very, very important paper. Maybe a book or booklet. It might even be something like a scroll. Pussy didn't tell me what it looked like, just what was on it, so I'll know it when I see it." Foxy quickly explained. "Did you ever see her with something like that?"

His head started shaking before he answered. "Nope. Not that I can think of, anyway. Miss Katnip never seemed to do anything like that."

"What about…what about a large vat or maybe a, I don't know, a cauldron." Foxy felt her fingers twitching. "Did you see Pussy with anything like that?"

"Foxy, uh, what are you talkin' about?" Robby took a step backwards. Foxy took two forward to meet him.

"Oh, Robby, I'm sorry." She moved to press against him. "It's just…when I got that note and everything that came with it…. I've just been so scared. So worried." First pressing her hand against his chest, she slowly moved it in circles.

"Hey. Hey, don't you be scared." The feeling of Robby putting his hands on her shoulders raised the corners of her mouth. "You haven't been here too long, but Ms. Katnip, she's tough. Tougher than nails. I don't know how many times I thought she was done for, but she always comes through. And she's smart. Smartest person I know. I've never met anyone like her before."

Foxy pulled back and stared up at him. She fluttered her eyelids. "What about me, Robby? Don't you see any of those things in me?"

"Hey, you're somethin' else, Foxy. I mean, I don't think I've ever met anyone like you before, either. And Miss Katnip sees somethin' in you, too, or else she wouldn't have sent you that note and signed the club over to you." Robby's eyes almost sparkled. It was a look she'd seen before.

"Oh, I'm just a caretaker until Pussy makes it back, Robby," Foxy purred. "And you flatter me, but…but what about those other things. The strength, the toughness, the smarts. Do you ever think of me that way?"

"I think of you all the time, Foxy." Robby leaned down towards her. She never let him get close.

Both of her hands came up and she pushed herself away from him. Or more accurately, pushed him away from her. "This isn't a good time, Robby." She heard her own tone and quickly followed, "I mean, I'm just too upset right now."

"Sure thing, Foxy." Robby took another step back. "You want me to send someone up here to clean this place up?"

"No. No, not yet." In a slow turn she looked at the littered floor. "I want to go through it again. Make sure I haven't overlooked anything."

"You bet. We should have everything ready to go in a bit." He hesitated. "Are you sure you're gonna be okay to sing tonight, Foxy?"

"Oh yes," Foxy looked back at him, "I really want to sing tonight. I'm hoping that we have the biggest crowd ever, with everyone here just to hear me sing. I want to do this for Pussy. I want her to know just how well I've done with her in my mind."

"Uh, is everything okay?" Both of them turned to the voice, and Foxy was sure that Robby recognized it as clearly as she did. The petite form just inside the door stood with her arms wrapped around her midsection, staring over at them.

"Oh, Robin," Foxy said, "you couldn't have come at a better time."

"Are you sure? I mean, I could come back if you—"

"Nah, it's okay, sis," Robby moved away from Foxy, and towards his sibling. "I was just about to leave, and it looks like you really wanna talk to Foxy."

With a nod towards her, Robby walked away from Foxy. He paused briefly beside his sister, and Foxy saw his lips move. What he said to her was a mystery, though.

As Robby moved on, Foxy moved towards Robin, filling the void her brother left moments before.

"Are you okay, Sweetie?" She moved her hand over to rest on Robin's arm. At first touch, she could feel the young woman trembling.

Robin leapt to Foxy, wrapping her arms around her in a tight hug and pressing her head against Foxy's bosom. "Oh, Foxy! I ju-just wanted to be nuh-near you right now. I'm so scared." Tears soaked through the cloth, wetting Foxy's chest.

"Sweetie, Sweetie," Foxy purred softly, "it's okay. I'm right here."

The grip around Foxy tightened. Foxy brought her hand up and tenderly brushed her fingers through the red hair atop Robin's head. They stood like that for a full minute, until the sobs slowly subsided.

"You doing better?" Foxy asked.

"I…I'm just worried." Robin let her grip go and pulled back far enough for Foxy to see her face. "What if Miss Katnip doesn't come back? What are we going to do?"

"Sweetie," Foxy ran her fingers through Robin's hair once more, "we can't think that way. All we know is that whatever Pussy decided to do, she thought it was dangerous enough to take some pretty severe steps. It's why she signed the club over to me, just to be safe. Now, I hope it doesn't come to this, but if the worst happens, I am going to do everything I can to make sure that Pussy is left with the legacy that she deserves."

"Oh, I can't think about that." Robin turned away from Foxy, and her demeanor changed. She took a couple of steps deeper into the room. "Wh-what happened?"

Foxy moved on to the entrance to the room, closed the door, and quietly turned the lock. "I've been looking for something. I was hoping that maybe Robby knew something about it, but he didn't." A few steps brought Foxy back right behind Robin. "Is there any chance that you could help me?"

"What is it you need?" Robin turned around. Foxy stood above her, staring down into her soft blue eyes.

"I can think of several things," Foxy growled, "but what I was searching for, and what I was hoping you might know something about was…. Well, I don't know exactly. That's part of the problem. Pussy said I would know it when I saw it, and I wish I could tell you details, but it's likely going to be a piece of paper or group of papers. A book maybe. Have you seen Pussy with anything like that?"

Robin shook her head. "Not that I can think of. Miss Katnip was always here, though, so she never really brought anything into or out of the club. Nothing like that, anyway."

"Sweetie," Foxy brought her hands up and placed them on either side of Robin's face, "I want you to think hard about this. You're always at the door. You see everything that comes into or goes out of this place. Did you ever see anything—anything at all—that ever made you wonder what was going on?"

"I don't think so. I mostly just talk to the customers, Foxy. Make them feel welcome. It's what Miss Katnip always wanted me to do. She—"

"Stop!" A sharp tone rose in Foxy's voice. "Stop talking about Pussy, Sweetie. Just listen to me."

"Y-you're hurting me," Robin squeaked.

Immediately Foxy dropped her hands. "No! No, Sweetie, I'm not. I…I'm just a little frightened myself. I would never hurt you."

She saw Robin slip her hand up and rub on her cheek, all the while staring at Foxy.

"Honest, Foxy, I never saw anything strange that Miss Katnip brought in. She lived here, though, so she could have brought it in at any time, or even through the back so I didn't—"

"The back!" Snapping her head, Foxy looked towards the door to the room. "The kitchen. Why didn't I think of that." In a single swift motion, Foxy twisted back around and scooped up Robin under her arms. She lifted the petite woman up and drew her much closer, holding her still. "Oh, Sweetie, you don't know how wonderful I think you are right now."

Robin didn't meet her eyes. Instead, she was staring straight down. "F-Foxy, how are you doing this? You're holding me up like…like…"

"Like you were light as a feather." Foxy spun around, twirling the young woman with her. With a giggle, Foxy returned Robin to the ground.

"Are…what's going on? How did…?" Robin sputtered out a couple of questions, but Foxy barely heard her at all.

"Dammit," Foxy said. "It's too late to go through the kitchen right now. I'll have to wait until after we close."

A motion from the corner of her eye attracted Foxy, and her arm snapped out. Her hand wrapped firmly around Robin's arm.

"I…I need to get back downstairs. Get ready for opening." Robin's voice was barely above a whisper.

"No. I want you to stay up here with me." Foxy moved around, putting herself between Robin and the door. "Let's go have a drink."

With enough force to move the smaller woman along, Foxy stepped towards the bar in the room.

"Y-you're scaring me, Foxy. Please, I just want to—"

"Sweetie, I need you up here right now. I need you to help me." Foxy's hands moved up to rub Robin's shoulders. "You want to help me, don't you?"

"I want to go." Robin's answer was short and firm.

A strong smell filled Foxy's nose. It was a scent that she was far too familiar with, but this time it had a different flavor. "You are afraid," Foxy growled. "Good. That's a good thing. It's good to be afraid. It gets the heart racing and the blood pounding through your veins."

With a twist of her wrists, Foxy spun Robin around, looking her in the face once again. "It gets us back to our roots. Predator and prey. Hunter and hunted. The strong and…."

A long tear raced down Robin's cheek. Foxy stood still, watching it trail all the way off of her face and drop towards the floor. Foxy brought her hand up and broke the line of tears, letting them gather on her finger. That finger then moved up in front of her own mouth. Her tongue came out and licked it clean. The tears were a perfect balance of salty and sweet, and Foxy found herself grinding her teeth.

"Sweetie," Foxy said softly, "I'm sorry. I didn't mean to scare you like that. It's just that…that for the first time since this began with Pussy, I had hope. Adrenaline took over and I lost control there for a second."

"I…it's okay, but I still want to go," Robin snuffled her words, and Foxy could tell she was recomposing herself.

Foxy measured the moment, and reacted: she turned her back to Robin. Carefully practiced tears welled up in Foxy's eyes as she spoke. "I-I understand. My em-emotions always get the better of m-me. You don't have to stay here. You don't ever have to see me again."

The time between the end of her sentence and the fingers touching her back was less than five seconds.

"Foxy, Honey, I didn't mean it like that." The tone of Robin's voice was between regret and concern. "You did scare me, but, well, I guess I didn't take a minute to think about why. You don't have to worry, honest."

Quickly, Foxy turned around. Her eyes were kept slightly more open than natural, glistening with tears. "Really? You won't le-leave me?"

"Well, I don't see how I could right now. Not after the way I was when I came up here." Robin took hold of Foxy's hands. "It looks like we both need a little comfort right now."

"Oh, Sweetie!" Foxy moved in and pulled Robin into a hug. "Thank you. You don't know what it means to me for you to be here with me. Especially with everything that's happening. Who knows what else might go wrong? We need each other."

It wasn't long until Foxy felt Robin returning the hug in earnest. The tighter Robin squeezed, the more Foxy smiled.

Red is the Darkest Color

Brett Brooks

Chapter Twelve

The streets of Mutt Town were much colder than Pussy remembered. Especially at night. Which made the sight of the sun peeking above the horizon very welcome. The wind that came with it on the other hand, was not. She pulled the coat she borrowed from George a little tighter, and lowered the brim of the matching hat to shield her face.

Staring down, she continued her march through the city. She had a no clear destination in mind, and no decided path to get there. She let her feet and the city decide how that would happen. And the dim light of morning revealed to her that old habits die particularly hard sometimes.

Her feet shuffled and came to a rest. On the sidewalk in front of her was something that would easily be walked past a thousand times by a thousand people, none of them giving it a moment's pause. Five lines radiating upwards, forming a loose arc, set into the sidewalk while the concrete was still wet. Her head moved up and she squinted into the growing light.

"I know this place," she whispered.

Her head turned, staring across a street whose only cars were parked along its side. A small diner's lights stood out on a dark row of businesses. The only name above the door was the word "eats" written out in orange neon. The lack of automobile traffic aided in Pussy's decision to cross the street directly, and she wasted no time in stepping inside the restaurant. The room was warm, but she stopped cold.

Sights. Smells. Sounds. They all came back in short order. A young woman with nothing of her own. Coffee that had been brewing for hours on end hidden behind bacon and waffle batter. And laughter. More laughter than she ever heard before in her life. Pussy stood there, eyes closed and unmoving, letting it settle over her.

"You okay miss?" The voice was old, like the cracking of a tree limb in the wind. "You look a little lost."

"I don't think so," Pussy answered before opening her eyes to face the man.

"Don't think so, what? Don't think you are lost, or don't think you're okay?" He was shorter than she remembered, and his voice was a little more dry, but there was no mistaking that face. He was an old bulldog of a man, with deep set wrinkles that caused his face to sag, and one eye that was sunken away to nothing.

"Probably a little of both, actually," Pussy answered.

He looked at her, and she waited on him to figure it out. "Have we met, miss? You look awful familiar."

"I think that's very possible." Pussy pulled the hat off her head and shook her hair free. It tumbled down over her shoulders in a mess.

She watched his one eye grow wider. "Princess? Holy Mac! Is that you?"

"I haven't been called that for a very long time." She couldn't help but smile. "How are you doing, Joe?"

The air was almost forced out of her with the hug that answered. She would have laughed if a stabbing pain wasn't biting through her ribs. As gently as possible she pushed him back.

"I tell you, you are a sight for sore eyes. I never did expect to see your likes again!" Joe stepped away, but just to be safe she took a half step back herself. "Where you been? What happened after you left?"

"That is a very long story, Joe, and I would love to tell you the whole thing, but…but I…." The words failed her. She simply stared at him.

"Well, what brought you back here?" He took a step backwards and leaned against the counter. Pussy saw his body slump. Old muscles betrayed him, making him rely on outside support to keep him standing.

"Fate, I think." She glanced at the room. Four people. Two at the counter and two in a booth. "I'm surprised you're still here, Joe. It seems like everything else has changed."

He laughed. "I ain't goin' nowhere. I'm too old to change now. Besides, where would I go? This is my home."

"I think that's what you told me the day we met," she answered. "I'm sure you said that to every wet-behind-the-ears kid who wandered into this place, though."

"Don't sell yourself short, Princess." His finger pointed towards her, barely raised above his waist. "It don't take two eyes to see someone special when they come along."

"Flatterer." Pussy stepped towards the counter, taking an empty seat next to Joe.

"I mean it. Always did. You were one of the special ones. Still are, I wager." He stood back up under his own strength and began to wander to the other side of the counter. "This neighborhood is cheap living, so it always drew in folks who had nothing. Not a dime in their pocket or anything more than the clothes on their back." He nodded. "Lots of good folk, too. People I'm proud to think of as friends. But if you live long enough, you can see the difference between the folks who always will have nothing, and those that have something special."

"Well, I'm back here, so I guess I fall into that first category," Pussy chuckled.

She saw him look her over as much as he could from his position. "Looks like all you've got right now is the clothes on your back."

"Not far from the truth."

It took him a moment, but Joe turned and pulled out a pot of coffee. He placed an empty cup in front of her and began to pour. "What was it when you came here the first time? You were about this broke then too, right?"

"I…." Pussy hesitated. She stared at the cup, enjoying the aroma for the moment. "You know the story, Joe. I had no place to be and no one who wanted me. All I wanted was a chance. I got that here, and I made the most of it."

"You always had a chance," Joe answered quickly. "What you got here was a boost. All the folks here believed in you. Wanted you to get out of here and make it big. And from what I hear, that's just what you did."

Pussy pulled her head back. "Oh, really?"

He laughed again. "I'm old, not dead. Just about everyone around here's heard about Pussy Katnip. Beautiful singer who has her own swanky nightclub. First time I heard about her, I knew it was you."

"And just how did you know that, Joe?" Pussy brought the cup to her mouth and took a sip. Bitter as hell, just like she remembered. She upturned the nearby sugar container for a second, then began to stir in the sweetness.

He shook his head. "There was a reason I called you 'Princess,' you know. You never would tell me your name, and I never asked why. Figured you deserved that much, anyway. You ain't the kind of gal who comes along that often. There was something different about you. Folks around here looked up to you without knowing why. Took your advice. Saw you as someone who was here to help." She felt his hand rest on top of hers. "You were always meant for something better than this, Princess."

"I never thought of myself as better than this place," Pussy answered.

"Never said you did. We thought it, though." He leaned forward, resting against the counter once more. "Everyone who worked here with you knew it. We wanted it. Wanted you to get to where you needed to be."

"Maybe I should have stayed. I could have done just fine here, you know." The coffee cup went back onto the saucer with a soft clink.

"Heh. Gimme a break, Princess. Every shmo with a sob story who stepped into this place got something out of you. Free food. Money. Mostly just help, though." His lips smacked several times. "You needed someplace bigger. Something that would let you help out more folks."

"That's not me, Joe. I don't get involved. I just run a nightclub and entertain customers." Pussy set the spoon down beside the cup and let it rest.

"Sure ya do." Joe looked down at the counter and then back up. "You need something to eat, Princess?"

Pussy smiled. "I could go for a waffle. Just to see if they're still edible."

"You got it." He turned away from her. There were scars on the back of his neck, four of them, running parallel downward. "Nate, gimme a waffle with bacon."

"You got it." The voice belonged to Nate, Pussy assumed. A young woman, barely old enough to be working, walked out from the back. She glanced at Pussy and gave a half-hearted smile and then went to the couple at the booth.

"Be right up, Princess." Joe spoke and got her attention once more.

"What's with the neck, Joe?" she asked softly. "I don't remember those scars."

"That's because they weren't here when you were." His hand went to the back of his neck. "Happened just after you left. Maybe six months later. Nothing for you to worry about. It's long gone now."

"Who did it?" she asked anyway.

"Just a hustler looking to make money. I didn't agree and he kinda roughed me up a little. He figured out soon enough that there ain't no money in this part of town, so he took off." Joe shrugged. "It's okay, Princess."

A bell rang behind Joe. Like a reflex, Joe turned and grabbed it, and then put it in front of her before she could get a word out.

"What was his name, Joe?" She turned the plate, positioning the bacon on the left side.

"Eh, I didn't pay no attention to it. He was just a loser." His hand went to the back of his neck again.

"Really?" A light pouring of syrup dressed the waffle. "That surprises me, since you know the name of everyone you see more than twice."

Joe sighed. "Look, Princess, it's nothing. He's been gone for years. You look like you have other things to worry about."

"You're right, I do. That doesn't mean I don't want to know." She took a bite of the waffle. Warm vanilla and maple with a hint of cinnamon beneath. Her breath caught. "Mmmm. Good waffle, Joe. Damn good waffle."

"Like there was any chance it wasn't," he chuckled.

Pussy took a sip of coffee, staring at him the entire time. He turned away after only a few seconds.

"Fine." He looked back at her. "His name's Blaid. Lupo Blaid. But it don't matter. I hear that he moved to Big City. And good riddance, I say."

"Really?" Her eyes narrowed. "What did he look like?"

"Big fella. Wolfish." He shrugged again. "I dunno. He was scary enough, I guess, but I just…. He just didn't scare me. Seemed like he was out of place."

"Kinda like I did when I walked in," Pussy mumbled. She sat up a little straighter. "This is important, Joe, so tell me, did he ever ask about me?"

"About you?" He pulled his head away from her slightly. "Nah. Nah, he didn't…."

"What? What are you thinking?" she asked quickly.

"Y'know, he didn't ask about you, but...but he did keep wanting to see who was working each night. And he never seemed happy with it." Joe's face lost some color. "Do you know why he was here, Princess?"

"No. No, I don't, but I do know you need to do me a favor." She stood up from the stool, grabbing her hat and bundling her hair up under it. "You need to forget that I ever came back by here."

"Hey, I ain't gonna back down just because someone I care about is in trouble," Joe stood up as tall as he could, "that ain't my way."

"I know it isn't, Joe. And you'll never know how much that means to me," Pussy took a deep breath, "but there are people who are after me, and they know about you. About this place, somehow. I can't stay here, and I don't want you getting hurt."

"Yeah, but where are you gonna go? You comin' here tells me that you likely can't go back to your own house," Joe stated.

Pussy nodded. "You're right. I can't. I have to go someplace... new. Someplace they won't think to find me."

"Where?" Joe quickly hit his own chest. "You got a place here, I say. Let 'em come!"

"No. No, I won't do that to you." She wrapped the coat a little tighter around her. "And I can't tell you where, either. But I'll be back, I promise." She looked at the plate of food. "How can I stay away from those waffles?"

There was a moment of fight that she saw in Joe's eyes, but it didn't take long before the fire faded to concern. "You better come back. I'm betting you can't pay for your breakfast. You owe me money."

She pulled the hat down tight on her head. "You're right again. I don't want that kind of debt on my conscience." After taking a step towards the door she paused. "It was good to see you, Joe. I will be back."

"You're always welcome here, Princess." His voice turned soft and gentle. "Stay safe, you hear?"

"I'll do what I can." And with that she stepped back out into the cold night air.

Her feet knew the direction this time. She had only ever been that way by car, so the walk was a long trek. By the time she was in the right neighborhood it was well into morning. A few people wandered the streets. Mostly mothers out with children, either walking them to school or just out for a stroll.

It was possible that she was too late. That she was going to be forced to either wait the rest of the day, or make new plans. Of course, there was only one way to know for sure.

Forcing a nonchalance into her step, she walked down the street, still wrapped tightly in her coat and hat, despite the growing warmth of the day. His house had a handful of steps leading up to the door, and she mentally noted the large crack in the concrete that formed them. If this panned out, the very least she could do would be to give him a new set of stairs.

Her hand rapped against the wood of the door. After a moment she heard someone walking down the hallway. With a toss of her head she pulled the hat away so that her face was clearly visible. The lock turned with a heavy sound, and then the door swung inside, revealing the owner of the home.

"M-Miss Katnip," he stammered. "Wh-what are you doing here?"

"Good morning, Mr. Crocker." Pussy kept her voice calm and level. "May I come in? I have a huge favor to ask of you."

Red is the Darkest Color

Brett Brooks

Chapter Thirteen

The first time he ever stepped into the place, he was nervous as hell. He could hardly have been considered young, but he was still shy and inexperienced. At least in dealing with places like this. Give him a crisis—a burning building, a trapped child, a heart attack victim—and he was as cool as ice. Here? That was a different matter. The allure and talk about the club grew with every day, pulling in people from every walk of life. Including the fire department.

Instead of awkwardness and an uncomfortable night, the Kit Kat Klub offered up a relaxing evening of thrilling entertainment. He left that night at ease, and considered himself lucky enough to have found a place where he felt at home.

That was then, and this was now. George walked into the club with every nerve riding on an edge. His hand was damp with sweat, and he caught himself pausing at the top of the stairs. At a glance, the place seemed the same. The servers moved through the maze of tables without a hitch, while the band played music loud enough to drown out the next table, but not so much as to hinder the conversation across one. Robby stood behind the bar, slinging drinks and talking up a storm.

His sister, Robin, was back at the hat check, giving a gentle first impression to newcomers, and a welcome smile to regulars.

It was what couldn't be seen that nagged at George. The presence that wasn't here, and why. Pussy had told him that it was likely that Foxy would come for him. Send a goon by, or possibly even visit herself. He didn't like either option, so he chose his own. One that took the power and shifted the control.

He was here to see Foxy.

The idea was much better in his head before he got here. The story Pussy told him about her was intimidating, to say the very least. And now the same club that normally he found so inviting was difficult. Each step was almost painful, as though his shoes were suddenly laced with thorns.

Still, he took step after step, his head on a constant swivel. One after another until he found himself at the bar, sitting in the same seat he was accustomed to having. A friendly face appeared on the other side of the bar, and for a brief moment he felt relaxed once more.

"Hey, Chief!" Robby wiped the bar down in front of him, whether it needed it or not. "How you been? I suppose you've heard the news about Miss Katnip?"

Several thoughts ran through his mind, and he pushed each one back in turn. "I've heard something," he finally answered, "but no details. What's the story?"

"Well, that's a long one," Robby threw the towel over his shoulder, "but the short version is that Miss Katnip took off after Jenny, got into a bit of a twist, and left the keys to the store with Foxy."

"Did she?" George kept his voice calm and level.

"Yep. I'm not happy that Miss Katnip isn't here, and I'm worried to death about her, but Foxy is doing a great job," Robby continued.

"Is she?"

"She's a smart broad. Knows her way around a club, too. Miss Katnip couldn't have chose anyone better." Robby shifted his weight, as well as the towel from one shoulder to the other.

"Really?"

George almost jumped when Robby slapped the towel down on the bar. "Okay, Chief, what's the deal? I'm getting nothing but attitude from you with everything I say. You're sitting there acting like your about to snap your cap. Something wrong?"

He started to wonder if coming here was a bad idea. A forced smile grew on his face. "No. No, I've just been under a lot of pressure at work, and hearing that Pussy might be in danger...."

"I get ya. Don't forget that it's Miss Katnip that we're talking about. She's gonna be okay. Foxy says that Miss Katnip has a plan, and we just gotta trust her." Robby pulled back slightly. "Set you up with a double?"

"That'd be great," George confirmed with a nod. Robby turned away, grabbing a bottle from the back bar. Taking that opportunity, George scanned the room again, looking for a familiar face or, more importantly, a very unfamiliar one. The dull sound of the glass hitting the bar turned him back. If anything, there was a clear over pour in the glass, but he wasn't going to complain. His mood could use the extra help.

"Need anything else, Chief?" Robby asked.

The alcohol felt warm going down his throat, and he licked his lips once as he pulled the glass away. "Yeah, Robby, actually I did have a question for you. Has Foxy been doing anything that you consider a bit…odd?"

"Whatcha mean, odd?" The look Robby gave him was telling enough.

"Anything. Anything that made you wonder about it." George leaned against the bar, trying to close the gap between himself and the bartender.

The towel in Robby's hands twisted around a couple of times and then fell free. "Well, she has been a little…. She's been looking for something. I'm not sure what, but she's asked all of us about it. The worst part is that she isn't sure exactly what it is, either."

"Then how could you help her?" George asked.

"Pretty much what I told her," Robby answered, "but then, she's really just worried. You can see it in her face."

"Well, that's good to know." George brought the glass up and emptied it. His breath caught for a moment from the alcohol's effect.

"What's good to know?" The rich, silky voice froze him solid.

Every moment of his turn was like a snail moving through glue. There she was. Red dress complimenting her color perfectly. A long, sleek smile lying just below a perfectly placed beauty mark on dangerously gorgeous face. The deep black hair hid her right eye, but the left one burned into him. It only fed the fire of his anger that much more.

"Hello, George," Foxy purred. "It's good to see you."

"Foxy." George swallowed reflexively after he spoke. "Good to see you, too."

She gestured to the empty stool beside him. "May I?" He didn't get a chance to answer before she sat down.

"Of course," he answered anyway.

"How have you been, George?" She made a show of batting her eyes, and George felt himself tense up as she did.

"Busy. Keeping very busy." He looked back over the bar, but Robby was gone. Trailing along the bar, he saw him helping another customer at the far end.

"Aren't we all." Foxy's hand brushed against the bar, moving towards him.

"So, uh, I hear that you, um, are…running things here. For now." He pulled his hand off the bar and rested it against his thigh.

Foxy leaned back and cocked her head to the side. "George, you seem tense. Is something wrong?"

"Um, that…I don't know." His fingers began to strum softly against his leg.

She sat across from him, her smile never wavering. Every second that passed, George felt his body becoming more and more rigid, and he suddenly realized that he was clenching his teeth.

"Why don't we go up to my office and talk," Foxy broke the silence with a soft statement.

"Your office?" The words came out before George could stop them.

Her eyebrow arched upwards. "Oh, we definitely need to go talk, don't we." She stood up and offered her hand. "Come on."

George stood up on his own, ignoring her offering. "Lead the way."

She walked ahead of him, never rushing or hesitating. He saw her wave to a few customers, and quickly speak to an employee as they made their way to the stairs. As she ascended ahead of him, his eyes moved lower onto her body. Halfway up he cursed himself for letting them linger.

Once at the top, she went to the door and opened it, stepping to the side to let George enter. For a moment he considered waiting to go after her, but the fact that they were about to be alone was enough. He went inside.

The room looked barren. There was almost no furniture in the place, and it looked as though someone had recently cleaned it.

"Pardon the mess," Foxy said as she stepped past him, "I'm doing some remodeling. There were a few items that needed replacing."

"So I heard," George mumbled.

He scanned for a place to sit. There was only a single chair near the book cases, and then four stools in front of the room's private bar. Foxy walked to the bar, so he followed.

"Would you like something to drink?" She pulled a bottle from the wall and took out the stopper. "Pussy has excellent taste in liquor."

"I'm sure." Despite his non-answer, Foxy poured the drink and held it out for him. Reluctantly, he took it.

"So, you spoke to Pussy?" Foxy turned away from him and pulled down a bottle and glass of her own.

"I did." He held the glass in his hand, turning it slightly as he spoke.

She turned back with a wide smile. "Good. That speeds things up, don't you think?" She took a sip of her drink. As she pulled it away, her tongue came out and licked the edge of the glass, getting up the droplet that tried to run down the outside. "What did she tell you?"

"That you betrayed her. Stole what was hers and forced her out." There was a rising tension in his chest. "And that you were probably going to be sending someone out to get me, if you didn't come after me yourself, so I beat you to it. Here I am."

Foxy moved just enough to sit down on one of the stools, never breaking eye contact with him.

Then she let out a soft sigh. "And why would I do that? You've never done anything to me."

"To get at Pussy!" What was welling inside him began to trickle out, and George raised his voice.

"Hmm." She took another sip of her drink and set it down on the bar. "I could see that logic. So, tell me, do you know where she is?"

"I don't. She wouldn't tell me." The words came out staccato, with more deliberation than intended.

"Shame." She shrugged. "Oh well."

"Oh well?" He stepped forward and slammed the drink down on the bar. "Oh well? That's all you have to say? You beat that woman half to death! I was barely able to nurse her back to health, and even then, she was a mess when she left my house. It's a miracle that she was even able to walk."

"I know." Foxy's voice was still calm and even, and she took a deep breath to pause. "Still, what does that have to do with us? I know you care for Pussy, and I won't blame you for that. You don't know where she is, so there's no point in trying to find out from you. And, truthfully, I don't want to hurt you. So, there we have it."

"You hurt her! Not just physically, but also in trust. You… you…." He balled up his fists, but kept them at his side.

"I did." Foxy quickly answered. "And did she tell you why?"

He hesitated.

"No, she didn't, did she?" Foxy stood up, her dress falling open to reveal a long leg beneath. "Because she never took the time to find out. She had no clue who I was, despite everything that was done to me. To me!"

She was inches from him. From appearances, he looked like he was not only capable, but poised to break this woman in half. He knew how deceptive appearances could be, however.

"I care for her, Foxy. I do." He stepped away, letting his fists turn back into hands. "And you hurt her."

"George," her voice turned to warm honey, "I know you care about her. And I'm sorry that what I did hurt you, but that's a totally different matter. And…and I hate to say this, George, but…are you sure that Pussy cares about you the same way you do her?"

"What is that supposed to mean?" He barked back.

"Just that. Has she shown you the same affection that you've shown her? Or has she just been playing with you? Teasing you?" Foxy dropped her head slightly. "Tell me, have you ever been up here with her alone? Like you and I are right now?"

"I…what does that matter?" He almost snorted when he spoke.

"I'll take that as a no." She sighed again, almost imperceptibly. "I'm so sorry, George. You don't deserve that."

"Wh-what?" George shook his head, doing his best to free it from the confusion settling onto his brain.

"I said I'm sorry. That I feel bad for you." She almost laughed. "What? Did you expect me to attack you? To be some horrible creature that only wants to destroy everything?" The laugh turned to a grin. "I won't say that I'm sorry about that, because I'm actually glad that I disappointed you there."

"Y-you're making it out like you've done nothing wrong!" He pointed back to the door. "You're lying to everyone here! They all think that Pussy gave you the keys to this place willingly. You stole it!"

"I took it legally," Foxy corrected quickly. "And yes, I am lying to them. What do you think they would do if I told them the truth? Turn against me? Leave?" Her hand came up and wagged a single finger. "No. No, I don't want them to be out of work. I know how difficult that can be, struggling on the street with nothing. Those people don't deserve to be thrown out with the trash."

"So, Pussy is trash now?" George countered.

"Something like that, yes." She stepped closer. He stepped back. "George, I want you to be on my side. At the very least, I want you to not be against me. I need help here. You're not only in well with the employees of the Kit Kat, but you are also an important figure in the community. I want you on my team."

"What are you even saying? Are you hearing yourself?" George waved his hands towards her in small circles.

"Are you hearing me?" She countered. "It might surprise you, but I want many of the same things that Pussy was claiming to do. I want to clean up this area. I want it under control, and to make sure that the bad elements are kept out. And that all starts with getting rid of Pussy Katnip."

"You're insane," he whispered. "You're completely nuts."

"No, I'm not. Listen to me." She stepped in quickly, and George found himself with nowhere to retreat. Their bodies were separated by only a thin lining of air. "I'm a lot of things, George, I won't deny that, but right now I'm a woman asking for help. Asking for you to come over and help me accomplish some wonderful things for not just the people in this club, but for the city as a whole." Her hand came up and brushed against his face, and suddenly he could hear the sound of his heartbeat in his ears.

"Get out of my way," George whispered.

"I'm not going to, George. I need you here right now." He felt her breath on his neck. "I have a lot to offer you, and unlike Pussy, I'm not a tease." Something warm brushed up against him. "Tell me that you'll let me try to convince you, George. Tell me that you don't want this."

His breath became rapid and shallow. All the moisture escaped from his mouth as her body melded against his. Their combined weight pushed them back into the shelves behind George, causing him to collapse slightly.

"If you want my help," George muttered, "then back off, lady."

He counted a full five seconds before he felt her move. He thanked the stars that the movement was back and away. When she was beyond an arm's reach, he stood erect, rolling his neck and shoulders back. He brushed down the lapels of his jacket and tugged his sleeves back into position.

"I do want your help, George," Foxy purred, "and maybe, just maybe, you'll let that turn into something else."

"Don't push your luck." He hoped he sounded more confident than he felt. "I'm doing this to help Pussy. If I help you, then you have to leave her alone. Deal?"

"I need to talk to her, George." She raised a finger. "Just talk. I'm sure she'll listen to reason this time."

"No. No, if you want something, I'll talk to her when she shows back up. I don't trust you that much." George insisted. "And I won't do anything to hurt anyone. Nobody."

"I would never ask you to do something like that." Foxy took a step closer. Despite his first instinct, George stood his ground. "All I want is for you to keep coming in here, acting like everything is fine. Telling everyone that we had a good talk."

"That's it?"

"Well, unless you want to do something else." Foxy's slipped her tongue from her mouth like a snake. "Which I'm still more than game for, personally."

"I'll just have the drink, thank you." He kept his head high.

"Oh, that's a good idea." Foxy slinked to the bar and retrieved the two glasses, holding one out for George. He took it in his hand. It felt heavier than it had before. "Let's drink to it."

Foxy held her drink out, waiting for him to respond. After a moment he brought his up to meet hers, signaling their agreement with a crystalline chime.

"To our future." She brought her glass up and tipped the contents back, swallowing every drop.

George brought his to his lips and took a light sip. The whiskey was sharp and clean. Foxy was right, Pussy kept a fine quality up here. And now he was here, too. In with Foxy. Close to her. Able to keep an eye on her and keep Pussy informed. He could be Pussy's eyes and ears. Help her get the club back. It was a good plan. In his mind, it was a very good plan.

He looked at Foxy as she put the glass back down. Her one revealed eye gleamed in the light of the room. Perhaps a bit too much, actually.

And George began to wonder if he was in the position he hoped for after all.

Red is the Darkest Color

Brett Brooks

Chapter Fourteen

"Miss Pussy?"

Despite the shock in his voice, she couldn't help but smile. "Hello, Albert. May we come in?"

"Of course!" He backed out of the doorway as quickly as possible.

She had forgotten how big the door actually was. Even if Albert hadn't moved at all she and her companion could have passed through the entrance without even brushing against him. With the towering height of it, she almost felt like a child walking inside. That, more than anything, made her have to repress her emotion.

"How have you been, Albert?" Pussy asked, focusing on the positive standing in front of her.

"I've been doing very well, Miss Pussy. Thank you for asking." His eyes smiled more than his lips. "More importantly, how have you been? It's been…."

"Nine years," she finished for him.

The happiness on his face suddenly aged. "I was going to say 'too long.'"

"Well," Pussy sighed, "it's been that, too." The necessary question hung in the air. "Is…is she in?"

"She always is nowadays, Miss." The last vestige of joy left Albert's voice.

"How is she doing?" Each sentence became a little softer and lower.

"Some days are better than others. Recently it's been very quiet."

The shuffling of feet behind her caught Pussy's eye. "Oh, and I'm being rude." She moved to the side, giving the two men a clear view of each other. "Albert, I would like to introduce Mr. Todd Crocker."

"A pleasure to meet you, sir." Albert added a slight bow to his greeting.

"Oh, I, uh," Todd's eyes were in constant motion, "yes, it's nice to meet you, too."

"Mr. Crocker's helping me with some issues that I'm having right now," Pussy explained. "I was wondering if you might be willing to give him a tour of the house, or just take him to the study for a bit." Pussy looked down the hallway. "While I go pay a visit."

"Are you certain, Miss? Would you not prefer me to introduce you?" Albert asked.

"That's probably a very bad idea. I was always taught to pull the bandage off quickly." Pussy took a deep breath as she turned to her guest. "Mr. Crocker, if you need anything don't hesitate to ask Albert. He's the best."

"You flatter me, Miss," Albert said.

"It's only flattery if it's not true."

"You will find her in the conservatory," he informed her.

Pussy took a few steps down the hallway and then stopped to look back. Both men were staring after her. "Oh, and Mr. Crocker, ask Albert to show you the private study. I always liked it better than the public one."

She was certain they would have said something in response if she had waited. Still, she could hear their conversation as a dull noise that dimmed to nothing as she moved down the hall. And as they faded the surroundings did their best to swallow her whole.

The colors were more muted than she remembered. All the blues and purples were more vivid, more regal, in her memory. At the moment, she wasn't sure if her memory became brighter or the subject dimmer over the years.

Turning the corners with an ease that surprised her, she weaved her way to the back of the house, defying the temptation to stop and enter many of the rooms that beckoned her off course. Until, in far less time than she actually hoped, she stood in the doorway, staring into the massive space ending in a veritable wall of windows twenty feet high that looked out over the expansive gardens of the estate.

The room looked like she remembered. White walls with white filigrees latticed across it, creating more of a texture than anything. Brilliant white marble floors reflected the light from outside, illuminating the space in a near blinding light. The room looked the same, but the contents did not.

A single chair sat on the far side of the room. It was framed by the windows and the floor so that, from her perspective, it almost seemed to float in center of a great void. It's back was to her, so that the occupant could stare out the window. There was no table to its side, nor in front of it from what she could see. It was a cradle of isolation.

She couldn't move. Despite the commands she was sending towards her feet, they refused to obey. Instead, she simply stood in the doorway, watching. Staring at the silhouetted chair hovering twenty-five feet away.

Then, a shadow broke the plane of the outline. A faint hint of a profile.

"Pussy?" The voice was weak. It almost cracked with a single word. And it almost broke Pussy. "Pussy, is that you?"

"Hi, Mom." Still, her feet refused to obey.

A figure stood, first nothing more than another delineated shape extending from the chair, but the light of the room took pity on her, and the reality of the woman became clear. Her coat was a tawny blond, just slightly darker than Pussy's own, but the blond hair they shared was identical. Whereas Pussy's hair hung down just past her shoulders, though, her mother's hair barely came below her jawline.

"Oh, Pussy," her arms extended wide, "come here, child."

And that was what it took. Instantly, Pussy was walking forward, steadily faster, until she was next to her mother, and taking in her embrace—and then pushing away as the grip caused her to grimace and groan.

"You're hurt," her mother stated. "What happened?"

"It doesn't matter." Pussy stepped back. The woman in front of her seemed slightly smaller than she should have been, but her grip was still as fierce as Pussy remembered. "How are you?"

"I…I've been better," she replied. "I'm not the woman I used to be."

"You'll always be an amazing, woman, Mother." Pussy smiled, hoping that it looked somewhat genuine.

"Ah, if only that were so," she sighed. "My body is failing, you know. I…it would be nice if…."

Pussy felt her muscles clench. "I just came to talk to you, Mom."

"Oh, I know. And you don't know how thrilled I am to see you. It's been so long! I never meant to drive you away. I'm sorry, I just…."

"Don't." Pussy's hands balled into fists. "Please, mom, I just got here. Don't."

"You do have some, don't you?" She stepped back, leaning against the wingback chair.

Pussy spun on her heels. "This was a mistake. I knew it was a mistake, but I came anyway."

"Don't go!" Once more it seemed that Pussy's body responded more to her mother than herself. She stopped cold. "I wouldn't ask, Pussy, it's just that, well, you know that I can't make the potion anymore."

"Yes, and you know why." Pussy turned back. "You told me that this would happen. You knew it would. The gift passed from you to me, yet you won't accept it."

"It wasn't time!" She rushed forward, and Pussy's muscles tightened, ready to act. "There was still so much I could do. So many things I could accomplish."

"That's not how it works. You know that. Neither one of us has any control over it." Pussy's teeth were clenched tight.

"Oh, I know. I just want—I need—a little to help me through the day. To help me heal, Pussy. I need to heal," she pleaded.

"Mother, no. You can't. I just…I can't." The words were stressed.

Pussy watched her mother's head drop, and then slowly raise up. She was looking at her whole body.

"You're hurt," her mother said. "You're not healing. You don't have the potion. You can't make it anymore. Have you forgotten it already?"

"No, it's…it's complicated," Pussy answered.

"You have. You forgot." There was an audible huff as her mother stepped back.

Somewhere inside, Pussy heard something click. "How could I forget, Mother? You started teaching it to me when I was six. Or don't you remember that when I was ten years old you wouldn't let me have dinner until I could recite the whole damn thing back to you!" Her volume increased, moving from conversation to something much louder. "How many nights did I go to bed without food? Do you know? Because I don't. For a while I counted, but eventually I gave up. I couldn't see the point anymore."

"Then why don't you have any of the potion?" her mother shouted back. "You never appreciated its gift. You've never understood what it gave you. What it gives you!"

"I understand what it took from me!" Pussy wailed. "What it could take from me again if I'm not careful." She hesitated, but couldn't stop the words for long. "How could I forget my own mother going from this great hero whom everyone admired to a strange madwoman tearing at the walls, screaming day and night, begging me for something that she knew I couldn't give to her!"

Silence bit into both women.

"Who is Foxy Kitt?" Pussy asked.

Her mother stepped back as if she had struck her physically. "Foxy Kitt? I...I don't know that name."

"You do." Pussy whispered. "I was hoping you didn't, but.... Who is she?"

"I don't—"

"Don't lie!" She closed the distance between them. "You want to know what happened to me? She happened to me. And unless you help me, I'm not sure that there's going to be anything I can do in response."

"Pussy, I'm telling you the truth," her mother answered softly. "I don't know who Foxy Kitt is," she paused, "but I do know the name Vulpa Kitt."

"Vulpa Kitt? I don't...who is she?" Pussy took a step back, giving her mother room to speak.

"It's not...." She shook her head. "It was so long ago. There's no way that...."

"Mother," Pussy's voice was emphatic, "who is she?"

She turned away, and all Pussy could see was the back of her mother's head as she spoke out to the far side of the room.

"I lied."

Pussy felt her whole body lurch at the sound of those two words. "About what?"

"The story. The history." Her voice was fragile. "About us. About the Katnip family."

A wave of heat passed through Pussy. There were no words. She simply stood still.

"There was a time, the way it used to be, when it was…that it wasn't just our family line." Pussy saw her mother's right hand tremble slightly. "It was the time of Cedric the Bold, centuries ago, and the people needed help. They needed a champion. A potion was created to help them out and give them hope for the future. It was designed to give special powers to the imbibers." Pussy's mother licked her lips. "Yes, I said imbibers. For one person it would provide amazing mental abilities, giving them heightened senses and even glimpses into the future. For the other, it…it gave them amazing physical abilities. Strength. Speed. Everything."

An uncomfortable truth began to wash over Pussy.

"Our family—the Katnip line—gained the mental abilities. The physical gifts, those…those went to a different family. The… the Kitt family line. The secret was passed from mother to daughter, each family knowing their own secret, until…." Her mother stumbled over the words and then gradually turned back to meet Pussy's eyes. "It was so long ago. Before you were born. Before I even met your father."

It took more effort than Pussy imagined for her to say the next words. "What did you do, Mother?"

"It was…I mean, there was…. Vulpa. Vulpa was the same age as me. She was the descendent of the line. The…the other half. I was the inheritor of the mental gifts, she the physical. But," she shook her head, "we didn't want that. We thought we could do better. Make it better." A single tear traced its way down her face. "We knew the recipe then. We…I thought that I could fix it. Give the both of us the mental gifts and the physical, so that we were both complete. So that we could do twice the good. It…didn't work quite that way."

Pussy waited, but nothing was forthcoming. "Mother, keep going. Tell me."

"At first it was good. She…she was feeling her mind open up, and I was amazed by the physical side of things. I just…I never imagined anything like that. We were giddy, both of us. And then things started to change. Vulpa started to change. Her mind it…she started becoming less rational. More emotionally extreme." Black eyeliner sagged under Pussy's mother's eyes. "She went insane, Pussy. She attacked me. I'd never seen her like that. She was so strong. Possessed. I thought she was going to kill me." Her voice turned to a tin can scraping in the night. "I tried, Pussy, I really did, but I couldn't save her. She went insane. Lost touch with reality and just…. The last time I saw her she was going into the asylum. I checked in on her afterwards, but she was gone. I don't know what happened."

The figure of the woman standing in front of Pussy was one she had seen before, but it was at this point she realized that she had no idea of that woman's true identity.

"And you…you never told me this? Never thought I needed to know?" Everything Pussy could see was tinted red.

"What did you want me to tell you? How could I explain something like that?" her mother countered. "I had a bigger responsibility, and then when I thought you might be ready, you ran away."

"I never ran away," Pussy growled. "I was pushed out. There's a big difference."

"You took the potion and left. You knew I needed it—that I STILL need it—and you selfishly took it for yourself," Pussy's mother spat back.

"No. You know that's not true." Her eyes narrowed to slits. "But…you changed the potion. You…it took longer for it to affect you, but it did. You still want the potion. Your body—your mind needs it." Pussy could hear her own heart trying to beat out of her chest. "Mother, which version of the potion did you teach me? It was…I get physical gifts. I…you taught me the one that drove you mad." Her head jerked around, angling towards Mutt Town. "The one that Foxy is taking."

"You understand, don't you, Pussy? I loved you. I wanted the best for you and—"

"And you were willing to risk my life," Pussy interrupted. "Tell me, Mother, did you teach the formula to me because you wanted the line to continue, or were you already trying to find a way to keep it yours forever?"

"Don't talk like that, Pussy. I followed the Katnip tradition. I did what I needed to do," her mother answered. "Blood is thicker than water, after all."

"True," Pussy whispered, "and it also turns black when finally expose to air."

She spun on her heels and walked, moving with a purpose out of the room.

"Pussy, wait!" Her mother's words fell off of her as she walked away. "Pussy, don't leave. Don't leave me like this, please!"

The sound of her mother's voice became a droning noise behind her. It was entirely possible that she followed her down the hall for a while, but Pussy refused to pay notice. Her mind was focused on one reality. One future that awaited her, one way or another. Either Foxy would find her and end her, or she would fade away, living only for the hope of something long lost.

"Miss Pussy?" Hearing Albert's voice was a bucket of cold water. Pussy stopped and looked into the room, seeing Albert standing beside Todd Crocker in front of a long series of portraits. All women, each from a various age. The Katnip family line. Albert rushed towards her. "Miss Pussy, are you all right?"

There were too many answers in her head. Too many thoughts that had to be sorted through before she could actually attempt to give a proper response. Instead, she said the only thing she could. "Take care of her, Albert. Please. Because she can't, and I…I won't." Todd Crocker walked up behind Albert. "Are you ready to go, Mr. Crocker?"

"Sure. Yeah. We can go." He moved past her, heading to the door. Pussy looked at Albert, seeing the many questions he wanted to ask plastered across his face like a billboard on main street. And he kept them all to himself. "Goodbye, Albert."

"Goodbye, Miss Pussy." His voice was proper and clean, just like it should have been. "Please, do come back."

She walked out the door, hearing Todd following up as quickly as he could.

"Are…are you okay?" There was more concern than curiosity in his voice.

"I'm fine. Thank you."

"You don't seem fine." She saw him hurry to move alongside her, but said nothing in reply. So, he continued,

"Albert seems very kind."

"He's wonderful." There wasn't a shred of doubt in her mind.

"He showed me several rooms, including the private study. I was speechless. The whole house is just spectacular, actually. This must have been an amazing place to grow up."

Pussy stopped at the car, staring across the roof at Todd, who paused at the driver's side door. "I just spent my childhood here, Mr. Crocker. I didn't grow up until after I left."

She did her best to not slam the car door as she shut it behind her.

Red is the Darkest Color

Chapter Fifteen

There were dozens of pots and pans, most of which Foxy could barely identify. It was difficult, but she did her best to sort through them without making a mess, looking for any sign or evidence of unusual use. Everything looked used, but none of them looked like they had been used for anything besides cooking.

She stopped searching, as she had done many times throughout the night, and took a deep breath. Her eyes might have been failing her, so she put some hope into the idea that perhaps her nose would be more successful. Her eyes closed and her nose went up, taking in a slow, deep breath.

Nothing.

It took all of her self control not to smash the pot racks to pieces. Instead, she decided to take it out on a single pot. It was large—far larger than anything a person would use at home—and she snatched it roughly from the wire shelving. Placing it in both hands, she slowly pressed against the sides. The faint cry of metal, begging for forgiveness and then yielding to the devastating pressure filled the kitchen space.

Steadily she pressed on, seeing and feeling the metal collapsing under her hands. Her elbows raised up just as her hands came together. Shifting quickly, she turned the pot so that her hands were on the top and bottom—or what once were, anyway—and then applied new pressure. The sensation of the metal surrendering to her efforts brought a slight smile to her lips. Images of her hands crushing other things, from stones and bricks to her hated enemies, raced through her head, unbidden into her thoughts.

Her hands met a second time, and she held out the pot at arms length. Or what started as a steel pot, at least. The twisted metal in her grip could scarcely be identified by anyone at a glance, and it would take some effort for the common person to name after some examination. It fell from her hand and clattered against the floor, issuing an off key song of its own demise.

"Useless," she muttered aloud.

Brushing her hands against each other, she walked towards the large pantry. The pans might have been a dead end, but there must be ingredients. There is no way that Pussy could create the potion from nothing. The only logical place to keep what she needed was here. After all, she kept the Fizz in clear view the whole time.

"Boss?" His voice was slow and deep. "Uh, Miss Boss?"

"Mugsy?" Foxy craned her head, trying to spot the body that went with the voice. "Mugsy, what are you doing here?"

"Miss Boss?" She walked towards his voice, and apparently he did the same towards hers. Soon enough she spotted the large figure of a man working his way awkwardly through the kitchen. "Oh, hi Miss Boss."

She stopped, waiting for him to walk all the way to her. "Hello, Mugsy. Let me ask you again: why are you here?"

"Oh, well, I was givin' you a report, like you asked me to," he answered.

"I asked you to?" Foxy crossed her arms and narrowed her eyes slightly.

"Yeah. You said that you wanted me to keep you informationed about finding Pussy Katnip." He nodded quickly. "Well, I wanted to tell you that I ain't found her."

A quick mental note was made by Foxy to make sure she clarified all of her instructions. "Yes, well, I meant for you to tell me if you had found her, not just that you were still looking for her." Her head turned slightly. "Mugsy, how did you get into the club? We've been closed for over an hour now."

He pointed back over his shoulder with his thumb. "The front door was unlocked."

Without giving a reply, Foxy pushed her way past Mugsy and walked briskly towards the front of the club. Her head swiveled about as she made her way through the main room, looking for anyone or anything out of place. The lights were dimmed, taking the majority of color from the room and leaving a cool blue tint to everything. Even in that odd color, there was nothing unusual to be seen. With nothing spotted to slow her down, she quickly reached the front door. Like Mugsy suggested, it was unlocked.

"I would swear that I locked this tight," she mumbled.

"I didn't unlock it, Boss. Honest," Mugsy promised from behind her.

"I believe you," she replied. Foxy took a moment, both for herself and to make sure that Mugsy was actually paying attention to her. "Now, Mugsy, I want you to continue to search for Pussy. And this is the important part, when you find her I

173

do not want you to permanently damage her, is that clear? I do, however, want you to beat her to a pulp. Hurt her. Make her feel weak. Can you do that?"

The big wolf scratched behind his ear. "I dunno, Miss Boss. Every time I've ever tried to put my mitts on her, she's beat the tar outta me."

"She won't this time." A shadow fell over Foxy's face. "That isn't to say she won't be a fight, but she won't have the same edge you've seen her have in the past. She'll be soft, and ready for you to manhandle. And that's exactly what I want you to do, got it?"

"Uh, sure Boss. I guess I can give it a whirl." His words sounded more confident than he looked.

"Just do it, Mugsy." She opened the door a crack, feeling the cold night air brush over her leg. "Oh, and don't come back until you have something to tell me about her, okay? That doesn't include coming to tell me that you have nothing to tell me about her, either."

"Yeah. Okay, Miss Boss. Sorry about that." Mugsy moved past her to the door.

She opened it fully, letting him pass through. "Don't think twice about it—even if you are able. Just don't do it again."

"You bet, Miss Boss, I'll—"

The door closed in his face. This time, Foxy made sure that she locked it tight before turning and heading back into the club. Her pace slowed considerably when she saw what, or rather who was waiting.

A figure stood at the top of the short stairs, dimly lit from behind. She recognized her immediately.

"Is that true?" The voice from the figure barely found a way out. "Tell me what I heard isn't true."

"Robin." Foxy turned her voice into honey. "Robin, sweetie, I'm not sure what you heard, but—"

"That was Boss Dogg's man. His thug. And…and he called you boss." She sobbed openly. "And you told him to hurt Miss Katnip."

"Robin," she held her hands out, palms up, "we need to talk about this. It's not as simple as you think."

"What's going on, Foxy? You said that Miss Katnip was…that she had…." She could see Robin begin to physically tremble. "Who are you?"

"I'm Foxy. You know me. You know us." She took a ginger step towards the smaller woman. "Let me explain, please."

"Explain? How are you going to explain what you said. It was clear. You told him to hurt Miss Katnip. She's…. Miss Katnip took Robby and me in when we had nothing. Had nowhere to go. Why would you want to hurt her?" Robin didn't move.

One more step closer to her. "That's just one side of her, Robin. Everyone has different sides. Different things that make up who they are. Pussy has just shown you the one side."

"And what has she shown you that makes you want her hurt?" Tears streamed down Robin's face.

Foxy reached her hand out, moving it towards Robin's face—who turned away in a flinch, like oil moving from water. Foxy pulled her hand back slowly.

"Robin," Foxy's voice went dry, "do you trust me?"

"I…I…"

"Do you think that I trust you?" She turned the question back before it was answered.

Robin stared at her. "I th-thought you did." Her head shook slightly. "But I…I don't know. I'm not sure you—"

"Not sure I what?" Pulling her shoulders back, Foxy stared back with steely resolve. "Shared more than just a little special time with you? Brought you close to me?" Once more she brought her hand up. "I care about you, Robin."

They stood apart, with only a shadow separating them. "I…I wanted to surprise you," Robin muttered.

"You did," Foxy answered. "I wasn't expecting anyone tonight."

Robin's arms opened, and she slid her hands down her sides. Her eyes followed until she was staring at the ground. "I was… talking to Robby. We talk a lot, actually. He noticed that… that I've been acting different." She looked up. "In a good way. Different in a good way. I…I told him that I was interested in someone, but I didn't want to say who." Robin licked her lips and then pressed them tightly together. "He told me that there was someone he had been spending time with, too. He said it was you." Robin took a quick, short breath. "Is that true?"

Foxy considered her answer before speaking. "Yes. Yes, it is true."

Her words hit Robin hard enough to cause the young woman to stagger back a step.

"Would you rather I lied to you?" Foxy answered. "You wanted the truth, didn't you? Well, let me tell you the whole truth." She took a step towards Robin, feeling as though she towered over the other woman. "Pussy didn't give me this club. I took it from her. I threw her out onto the street in a heap, and I don't want her back here. If she does come back, there's no promise of what I'll do to her. What's more, I want something else that Pussy's family stole from me—from my family—many years ago, but I can't find it. It's my birthright. She's hidden it here in the club."

"Y-you're—"

"I have no intention of hurting you, your brother, or anyone else who works here, but I will tell you that I will not hesitate to do what I need to get what I want," Foxy didn't wait for Robin to answer. "That includes making sure that some people think that I'm more interested than I really am." She grabbed Robin by the arm and felt the other woman's arm go limp. "Men are disgusting. They are beasts and monsters and nothing that I— or you hopefully—are interested in, except to use for my own gain. And yes, that includes your brother. He might be better than most, but he's still a man. He's still has that same look in his eyes. When he sees me he only sees one thing. Well, I let him see that, and I'll take what I need while he's distracted."

"Ro-Robby isn't—"

"He's a man!" Foxy growled in Robin's face. "They are only interested in one thing that women have, and if they can't get it then you are less than nothing to them. I'll never let myself be used by a man ever again, do you hear me?" The sensation of her fangs poking out ran over her face. She ignored it. "This is my place now! I'm the boss! Everyone will do what I tell them, or else pay the consequences. If any man thinks they can take me, well, let them try."

"Y-you're hurting me," Robin whined.

"No, I'm not," Foxy countered. "I'm telling you the truth, and that's sometimes painful. But I'm not the type to hurt women." She relaxed her grip. "You...you should know that I'm...I'm here to do good. My family has always been the champion of the…the repressed. The people who need help. That's what I want, Robin. I want to help. Please, let me help."

"Help who?" Robin whispered.

"You! Everyone here at the club. Everyone!" Foxy answered in a heartbeat.

"That…that's what Miss Katnip does." Robin's voice was barely audible.

"Pussy is a thief!" Foxy felt a warmth rushing over her. "She pretends to be something that she isn't and lords it over everyone with a smug smile. Well, she understands the situation now. She knows what it means to be helpless."

"Miss Katnip isn't like that. She only helps people. Miss Katnip—"

"Stop saying her name!" Foxy's hand flashed in front of her. When it impacted against Robin's face, she hardly felt it herself, but the blow was strong enough to spin the other woman to the floor.

Foxy stood over her, staring down. Her mind raced through the past few moments, replaying out what she had done. Even as Robin began to turn over, Foxy crouched down beside her.

"Robin! Sweetie! I'm so sorry. I don't know what happened. Are you all right?" Her hands moved down to touch her, but stopped short. Hovering above Robin like some invisible shield prevented her from getting any closer.

"Get away from me," Robin spat. "I'm leaving."

Several thoughts hit Foxy at once, not the least of which was Robin returning to her home and explaining what happened to Robby. Explaining everything to Robby. And then Robby would tell others. And then….

"No." Foxy felt a chill. "No, Sweetie, you won't be leaving. You need to stay here."

Robin scooted back. "Just watch me!"

Grabbing hold of Robin's leg, Foxy pulled her back easily, bringing her almost face to face. "It's okay, Sweetie. I'll just… just keep you here with me. You'll be safe here. Away from everyone who might want to hurt you. I can protect you."

"Let me go!" Her hand was a blur as it moved, slapping Foxy hard on her left cheek.

Foxy smiled.

"I understand. It's okay. You'll understand in time. I know you will." With one hand grabbing hold of Robin's arm, Foxy stood up, pulling the other woman to her feet. "This is for the best, really. This way we'll be able to stay together. Grow together."

Robin screamed something, but Foxy chose not to hear it. She picked the woman up and threw her over her shoulder and began to walk towards, and then up, the stairs to the apartment.

"Don't be afraid," Foxy said calmly, "I'm not going to hurt you. I would never hurt you. You're going to be happy here. Here with me."

Robin continued to rain blows down on Foxy's back. "It's okay, Sweetie. I know you're scared. I would probably be scared, too, but you don't need to be. This is just…just a hiccup. It'll be done in a jiffy and then we'll be happy again. You'll see."

It sounded like Robin might be crying now. Foxy did her best to be gentle as she carried her inside the apartment, heading towards the bedroom.

"Now, this might seem a little harsh at first," Foxy explained, "but you'll see. It's just until you calm down and everything gets smooth again." She carefully took hold of the bedroom door as she stepped through carrying her package. "Everything is going to be just fine."

The door closed with a soft, gentle click.

Red is the Darkest Color

Brett Brooks

Chapter Sixteen

With the exception of the single light shining behind the bar, the entire club was dark. He preferred it that way.

The bottle in front of him was two-thirds empty. It was full when the night started, and if he had things his way it would be empty before he went to sleep.

"Damn broad," Boss Dogg muttered into the glass just before it hit his lips. He polished off the small amount that was left and set it down with a sound that echoed to the back of the club. Almost through reflex he picked up the bottle and began to pour. He didn't stop until the glass was almost full.

"She thinks that I'm some coward. Some…some punk that she can push around however she likes." He was looking straight forward, but focused on nothing. "I was important while she was still in diapers. There used to be a time when a man like me had respect."

"Are you sure about that?" He turned at the sound of her voice, but made no other significant move.

"Hiya, Pussy. Have a seat." The glass made its way back to his mouth.

She saddled in beside him. He could see her cautiously taking the stool to his right. "Probably not real smart, you comin' here and all."

"Why do you say that?" She spoke in the same annoying calm voice that he had come to despise.

"You're a wanted woman in these parts." He gestured vaguely. "Foxy—oh, excuse me, Boss Foxy—wants to be told if you show back up anywhere."

"I'm not surprised. She's likely getting a little on edge by this point," Pussy stated. "So, are you going to turn me in?"

Boss Dogg let his head lol to the side until he was facing her. "Hell no. That dame can go screw herself as far as I'm concerned." He slid the bottle over towards her. It wasn't until she grabbed a glass from behind the bar and poured herself two healthy shots that he was surprised.

"I came here to talk to you about Foxy, Boss." She took a modest sip from the glass.

He chuckled. "Not 'Boss' for me anymore. Foxy made it a point to take that from me. Just Dogg now. Or John Dogg, if you want a full name."

"Do you mind if I call you John?" There was an uncomfortable sincerity in that question.

"Go right ahead. I can't stop you." The glass beckoned him for another drink. "Never have been able to, actually."

"Well, that's actually what I wanted to talk to you about." Pussy pushed the bottle back near him. He didn't mind.

"Me stopping you?" He couldn't help but laugh. "Sure, go ahead."

"No. Well, not exactly anyway." He saw her turn to face him out of the corner of his eye, but didn't feel the need to reciprocate. "I want to talk to you about helping me."

That was enough to raise an eyebrow. A slight squeak accompanied him turning on the stool to face her. "You? Want my help?"

"It's more I need it, John." He watched her swirl the drink in her glass. It spun like a roulette wheel hoping for double zero. "We both want the same thing: Foxy gone. The only way that's going to happen is if we work together to achieve it."

His finger gently tapped the edge of his glass. "So, let me see if I got this straight. You want my help to get rid of Foxy, who has been working with me, so that I can help get your club back and set you up to be a pain in my ass again. That about it?"

"Sums it up, yes," she answered.

"And just what makes you think that I would want that?" His chest puffed out. "What makes you think I need your help, anyway? You been spying on me, Pussy? Is that what you've been up to?"

"Actually, no." In response, she seemed to puff up a little herself. "I just know you, and I'm starting to understand her, so let's just say that certain things added up."

"And one of those things is you and me becoming an equation," he said. "Well, I hope you aren't expect any number higher than two. She's got Mugsy in her pocket."

"I'm not worried about Mugsy. I didn't go to him for help, either. You're the one I wanted to talk to." Pussy leaned against the bar, scooting on her stool slightly as she did. "He wouldn't be any help, in any case. I need information, not muscle."

"And just what information are you expecting me to have?" His hand began to turn the glass in a circle on the bar top.

"You remember Jenny? The singer at my club?" Pussy asked.

"Sure. Tried to hire her away from you a couple of times," Boss Dogg admitted.

"She's being kept at a seedy joint over in Big City." As she spoke, he was hearing a little more venom in her voice. "And she didn't want me to do anything to get her out of there because someone—and I believe that someone is Foxy—has her kid sister shanghaied. You know anything about that?"

"I might." He raised a finger, pointing it at Pussy. "But I never liked it. Not the kid sister part."

"What do you know?" He had heard this tone from her before, and knew that wasn't actually a question.

"Not as much as you think." He took a big drink from his glass. "It was Foxy's idea, sure enough, to get you interested in hiring her by getting rid of Jenny. My plan was to trick her out of town. Send her off to the west coast on a wild goose chase. Foxy didn't like it. Not certain enough. So, she came up with the idea of getting her to some club she knew in Big City. Said she knew the guy who owned it. She wanted us to nab her and run her over there. Simple enough snatch and grab."

"So you didn't mind kidnapping her?" Pussy growled at him.

"It was just business, and also just a temporary thing. I figured she'd be out of there in a week, two tops," he explained. "And I didn't know bupkis about her kid sister. When Mugsy and I came back from Big City, Foxy explained that she had insured that Jenny would stay away indefinitely." He drained his glass dry. "I shoulda seen what was happening then."

"Do you know where Jenny's sister is being held?" He couldn't really blame her for her tone.

"Not exactly, but I got an idea. She's got Mugsy out at an old place over at the corner of Leonard and Short. A run-down brownstone. I can't remember the number, but it'll be hard to miss." The second his glass hit the bar he had the bottle turning up and pouring a new fill.

"And you think she's there?" Pussy asked.

"Well, Foxy is sleepin' over at your club, so there has to be somethin' keeping him there." He looked at the bottle. There was probably one more good glassful in left.

"Is there anyone there besides Mugsy?" Pussy's fingers tapped on the bar. He didn't know whether that meant she was angry or nervous.

"Beats me." His hand copied hers, fingers strumming on the counter. "I don't get told nothing anymore."

She sat there staring at him. A burning sensation formed at the back of his eyes, and he turned his head away.

"When Foxy finds out—and she will—you know that you're in trouble, don't you, John?" He felt her words on his shoulders.

"Well, I guess you better hurry up with whatever it is you're going to do, then." Boss Dogg tasted bile as he swallowed.

"You might want to lay low for a couple of days. One way or another this will be over soon." Pussy stood from the stool. She didn't make it very far away before stopping. "One question: why are you helping me?"

Underneath it, Boss Dogg heard the deeper question. "I don't like you, Pussy. You're pretty much everything that I've always hated wrapped up into one pretty package." He took a moment to form the words in his mind. "Still, I know where I stand with you. You're never going to do something out of left field, or cross me over. We don't see eye-to-eye, but we're square."

He saw Pussy move slightly, and for a minute he thought she was coming back over to him, but she wasn't. Words came from the darkness as she disappeared from view. "Thank you, John. You might not want to hear this, but you're doing the right thing. And don't forget what I said. Disappear for a while."

"I ain't got nowhere to go," he muttered.

No reply came, only the faint sound of the side door closing. He waited to make sure that no new figure stepped out of the shadows, and when he was content he turned back to the bar.

A face appeared across from him. The dark, hollow features looked beaten and crushed. No bruises showed, but there was enough abuse in the eyes and the corners of the mouth to make up the difference.

He'd never seen himself look like that before.

Reflexively he grabbed the glass and picked it up. It hovered halfway between the bar and his mouth. His eyes were looking past the glass at the bottle. A fifth of whiskey all but gone, and he had almost every drop.

The glass fell from his hand—or he might have thrown it. In either case he heard land behind the bar, shattering into fragments. A moment later he pushed the bottle after it.

He heard a sharp cracking sound as he stood and raised himself up to his full height. His right hand slipped inside his coat, returning with the short stub of a cigar that had seen much better days. He studied it for a second before putting it down on the bar.

The brief idea of cleaning up the mess he made behind the bar ran through his head, but that chore could wait until morning. He strode over to the door to his office and stepped inside without hesitation.

That's where he kept his cigars, after all.

Brett Brooks

Chapter Seventeen

The seat was uncomfortable. Repositioning and adjusting wasn't making any difference, but it didn't stop him from constantly doing it in the hopes of finding some form of relief. Normally, it wouldn't have bothered him, but this was the place where he always sat. Where he always felt relaxed and welcome. This was his seat.

"What's buzzin', cousin?" With the same smile and effervescence that was his trademark, Robby approached him.

"Hiya, Robby." He did his best to make the words sound happy. Calm. He wiped his palms against his pants.

"You want your regular?" Robby move over in front of him, hands on the bar.

"Yeah. Yeah, sure. That sounds fine." Every few seconds he scanned the room, looking and watching, waiting for the moment that he knew was coming.

"So, what brings you by tonight?" Robby already sat his drink down, well before he finished scanning the room.

"Uh, just the usual, I suppose." He didn't touch the drink. "Y'know, wanting to spend some time at the club."

"Uh-huh." Robby lingered on the other side of the bar. "Normally I know exactly why you're here, but Miss Katnip is still away, so…." George turned towards him, ready to defend himself if needed. "You doin' okay, Chief? You're actin' a little squirrelly. Again. This is two times in one week you've been like this."

"What? No, I'm fine. Just…just worried, I guess." It was a half-truth.

"Ah. Well, that's what a good bartender is for." He leaned over the bar, getting much closer. "What's buggin' ya, Chief?"

"Oh, I'm sorry. Sorry. Nothing. I'm fine. Honest." As casually as he could manage, he looked around the room. "Uh, have you seen Foxy tonight?"

"Sure. She's been running all over the place." He craned his neck up, looking throughout the club. "Can't see her at the moment, though."

"Where was the last place you saw her?" George felt himself chewing on his bottom lip, and did his best to stop immediately.

"She went into the back dressing room. I guess she must be getting ready for her set." Robby glanced at the watch on his wrist. "Yeah, she's due on stage in less than five, actually."

"Oh, that's great." George looked over his shoulder at the stairs casually winding up to the second level of the club. "I…that is…. Look, Robby, I've got to go do something. If for some reason Foxy comes out here, just…just don't tell her that I'm here tonight, okay?"

"Sure thing, Chief. Why? What's the story?" Robby replied with a furrowed brow.

"Stuff you don't want to know. Trust me, it's best that I don't tell you." George quickly stood away from the bar. "I'll be back soon enough, anyway."

"No problem, Chief. Do me a favor, though, and relax. You're jumpier than a frog on a frying pan." There was a sincerity in Robby's voice. That wasn't good.

George forced a smile on his face, turned away, and mentally cursed himself for not having the strength to hide his emotions.

The walk to the stairs took forever. Every step was like pulling his foot from a mud pit that was trying to suck him down. When he put his foot on the bottom stair, it was worse. It felt as thought an electric shock hit him with realization. The lower stairs were hidden from view, but as he moved higher, he would be visible. Not overtly, but if anyone looked towards the stairs, he would be out in the open.

He told himself not to run. And to the best of his knowledge, he didn't. Running would do nothing but draw more attention, so he kept it steady all the way up. All the way to the door to Pussy's room—Foxy's room right now.

The door was unlocked, but the handle still felt red hot in his hand as he turned it. Inside, the room was dark when he entered it, but as his eyes adjusted he noticed the small lamp lit in the corner.

"Damn it," he cursed under his breath.

No light meant little saturation, and the only real thing he knew about what he was looking for was the color. In the dark, red could disguise itself as dark blue, dark green, or any dark color for that matter.

He had no choice. His hands found the switch and with a flick of his finger the room was bathed in light.

Wasting no time he moved quickly to the bar. Every bottle that he looked at caused him to move his hands towards it, hopeful that it was the one. One after another they all went past, until he was at he last bottle, which also failed to deliver.

"Damn it. This can't be right." A second pass left his hands much lower, though still ready to reach out. Ultimately, it met with the same empty results.

He turned slowly, taking a slight step to his left each time. Before he could even make a half circle he stopped. On the small table beside the wing chair was a crystal looking bottle half filled with a distinctive red liquid.

It almost looked like he leapt for the bottle as he ran to it. Taking hold, he moved the decanter to eye level. It was actually fairly low. Maybe a quarter of a bottle left. His jaw clenched and eyes narrowed. Immediately he looked back towards the bar where he began, and then ran back to it. It only took a second or two to find what he wanted and grab hold of it.

With the bottle of gin in one hand and a glass in the other, he poured as much alcohol as the glass would hold. A couple of fingers worth remained. He got rid of it down his own throat. A rough cough followed him pulling the now-empty bottle away. Despite the burn running down towards his stomach, he had accomplished the task.

He set the empty bottle down and uncorked the decanter. The shaking of his hand caused a tinkling sound as he brought the two bottles together. Immediately, he moved them apart and took a long, slow breath. Once more he positioned the two. The tremble remained, but was decidedly less noticeable.

Very carefully he began to pour. It was a best guess scenario to be sure, but he transferred some of the red liquid—what he hoped was the Fizz Pussy had mentioned—into the empty gin bottle. It left about an equal amount of the Fizz in each of the two bottles, and then re-corked the gin bottle. All that remained was putting the gin from the glass into the original Fizz bottle to get it back up to the level he found. When he held the bottle out, it looked pretty close. Close enough, he hoped.

He put the bottle down on the table along with the now empty glass, and then grabbed the gin bottle of Fizz and went to the window. It was a high second story, but it had the long decorative ledge surrounding the whole building at that height. He pushed the window open, feeling the sharp bite of the winter air as it rushed inside. Through clenched teeth he leaned outside and placed the bottle on the ledge, as far away from the window as he could safely reach. There was no easy way to get to it now, unless you had a very long ladder. Which was actually something that was in his job description.

The window shut and locked as easily as it opened, and for the first time since he set foot in this room, George felt his lungs completely empty. He made his way back over to the bar and repositioned the bottles, doing his best to fill the empty spot by spacing out what remained. Turning back his eyes fell onto the table. The empty glass rested beside the bottle, which was definitely not what was there when he entered. A few fast steps brought him to the table and the glass, which he picked up immediately.

That's when he heard it. A moan, or a groan, or possibly even a low whimper, he couldn't be sure. The only certainty in his mind was that it came from beyond the door to his right. The one that led into the sanctum of Pussy's—or again, now Foxy's—bedroom.

He strained to listen, hoping that his ears were playing tricks on him. Robby said that Foxy had gone into the dressing room and not…. It happened again. The same sound, only this time a little more clear.

That wasn't Foxy. Her voice was deep and lush. This was a high pitch. And a tone he recognized from years on the job. It was desperation.

Carefully, he stepped to the door, moving his ear beside it. The sound was more consistent. A muffled whine—or maybe even a cry. The sound of trouble.

His hand surrounded the door knob and slowly squeezed. It gave easily, turning far enough to let him silently open it just enough to see inside.

What he saw froze his heart.

She was strapped down. Both hands tied over her head, with the rope then lashed to the headboard. Her feet were similarly bound, save for a length of wood between them keeping them parted slightly, and then that board tied to the foot of the bed. A gag was in her mouth, tied around the back of her head. Both of her cheeks were stained from tears. It was Robin. He knew that the moment he saw her, but it still took a moment to register.

And then his training kicked in.

He flung the door open wide and rushed into the room. The first place he went was to her hands. Free them and it not only would release a great deal of the tension that had to be working against her muscles, but it also might allow her to help get the rest of the knots untied. His fingers pushed and pulled, trying to pry enough of a gap to get a loose end started. Something to work from. That's when another whimper drew his attention.

There was pure terror in her eyes. The sort of fear that grabs ahold of someone and won't let go for any reason. It was the fear that now that he was here, he wouldn't get her free. That hope was about to be dashed. That her rescue was about to fade away and the nightmare would continue.

Not on his watch.

He shifted from using hands to using teeth. Biting down on the rope and pulling back with a better grip than his fingers could provide at the moment. He heard the faint sound of a squeak, but he couldn't be sure if that was the rope moving, or just shifting in his teeth. A second later he felt a shift. A pull on the rope. A gap.

His fingers snaked their way in, expanding the gap into a hold, and then pulling the rope loose one inch at a time. There was no need to untie it completely. As soon as it was relaxed enough Robin yanked first her left hand and then her right free. It took less than a second to free the gag from her mouth.

"Th…th…thank you." Her voice came out in short sobbing sounds. "Is Fah…Fah…Fah…."

"She's not here." He stopped her, giving her a chance to not say anything more. "And we're getting you out of her right now."

Both of them went to work on the binds around her ankles. These weren't as tight, and the one he worked on came free quickly. By the time he moved over to the other one, Robin had begun to loosen it as well, and he simply finished it off.

"Robin." He said her name firmly, but calm, getting her attention. "We have to go. Very quickly and very quietly. Can you walk?"

Her head bobbed quickly to the affirmative.

"Okay, let's stand you up." She took his hand and moved up to a wobbly upright position. It wasn't until this moment that he realized what she was wearing. The fabric was thin enough that she might just as well have been naked. "Hold on." He let go of her hand and quickly walked to the closet. The contents were a mess. Clothing was strewn about haphazardly, and some of it was ripped to shreds. He spied a robe of some sort and snatched it up.

"Here," he handed Robin the robe, "put this on."

It was almost painful watching her dress. Each hand shook so wildly that he was afraid she might not be able to get it through the sleeve. Eventually, though, she got the job done.

"Okay, here's what's going to happen." He looked Robin in the eyes, focusing her concentration. "I'm going to be a step ahead of you. I want you to keep a hand on my shirt. If something goes wrong, I want you to pull on it. If I feel you let go, I'm going to assume something is wrong, but that might take me longer, so try to pull, okay?"

Again, she nodded.

"Great. Now, stay close behind me. I'm gonna get you home." He smiled, and she did her best to smile back, but the only reason he saw it was because he wanted to.

His plan was simple. Once they were out in the open, visible to everyone, they'd be safe. Others would come to their aid. Robby would probably leap the bar and run up there. That meant they didn't have very far to go, but not far can sometimes be forever.

As soon as he stepped out of the bedroom he saw her silhouette in the hallway.

"I saw the lights on up here," Foxy said calmly. "I thought I might have forgotten to turn them off for a second, but then I remembered doing it. I didn't want extra light to disturb anyone."

His arm went back, shielding Robin. She had already moved in to press against his back, and the soft sound of her whimper had returned.

"Foxy, I need to get Robin out of here. She needs a doctor." Despite his desire to scream, he kept his voice soothing. "Step out of the way."

"Oh, no, you don't understand," Foxy began to walk slowly towards them, "I'm protecting her. She's safe up here. I'm keeping her safe."

"You had her tied up!" The volume on his voice went up more than he intended.

"She was going to run off. That wouldn't have been good." Something gleamed around Foxy's mouth. He hoped it was her lipstick. "You understand, don't you?"

"Foxy, if you really want her to be safe, you'll let me take her to see a doctor. Let us pass." He took a step forward. Before he could blink she was there, right in front of him.

"You shouldn't have come up here, George." Foxy whispered. "I needed your help and now…."

He lashed out, throwing his fist towards her head from well behind his body. She caught it while it was still two feet away from any impact.

"I really wish you hadn't come up here, George."

The last thing he remembered seeing was her fist heading towards his face.

Brett Brooks

Chapter Eighteen

"Do you understand the plan?"

He nodded back at her, just not very convincingly. "I don't think it's a good plan. I should be going up there with you."

Pussy lowered her chin, looking up from below her eyelids. "I need you here, Mr. Crocker. You are an unknown quantity. Once I have her, you'll be able to keep her safe."

"But if you don't get back with her—"

"If I don't get back with her, I want you to leave here and go be with your family," Pussy interrupted. "You owe that to them, and to me."

His fingers tapped the top of the steering wheel. She saw him shift his eyes to the left, looking out the front window at the building down the street. "I don't like this plan. You could use my help."

Turning to look out the front window, Pussy stared at the brownstone. "You are helping. Being here for me is a lot of help. Plus," she held her clutch over the back seat of the car, "I need you to hold this for me."

"What is it?" he asked.

"A temptation. I don't need it with me right now." Pussy let go of the clutch as Mr. Crocker took ahold of it.

He opened his mouth, she presumed to protest, but all he did was close it slowly.

"Thank you," she said. "Now, when I come out, if I have her with me, I want you to pull up to the front door. That way I know you are ready to go."

"I can do that," he answered.

"I'll see you soon." She was out of the car before he could respond. The wind ripped past her, bringing a sheet of snow with it, and threatening to rip the coat off her body. She turned the collar up, tightened the belt, and made her way down the street. The snow passed through the light of the street lamps, creating brilliant displays of white against the dark of the night.

Seven steps led up from the street to the front door of the brownstone. She covered them in three strides. Without hesitation she knocked on the door and stepped to the side. A few seconds later she heard the sound of metal sliding on metal, followed by a voice. "Who's there?"

Lowering her voice as much as possible and adding a raspy edge, she answered, "Foxy sent me."

If he was smart, he would ask to see her. Tell her to step out of the shadows to the side and into direct view. The sound of the door lock turning revealed his intelligence.

She only saw his wrist, but it was enough. Long before he had the door open wide, Pussy grabbed the man's wrist and yanked the arm forward. The man fumbled with the door, trying to get it open, but he wasn't quick enough and his face smashed into the edge. The sound of bone crunching—likely his nose—

wasn't enough, so Pussy pushed his arm back slightly, and then pulled again with all her might. After the second impact, she felt the body on the other side go limp and slump down.

Her shoulder went into the door, and it gradually gave way, eventually offering up enough gap for her to squeeze through. Upon arrival inside, she dropped to her knees, making sure he wasn't going to get up anytime soon. She stood back up and closed the door as quietly as possible.

"What was that noise?" It was a little late for quiet.

The voice came from upstairs. Just beyond view from the sound of things, leaving her no time to get up to him. She'd have to wait, so she moved down the hall a few steps.

"Leon, I asked what…." Quick footsteps tumbled down the stairs and a large figure ran into view. Much larger than the first guy.

He said nothing, but his hand pulled something from his pocket. She didn't wait to find out what it was.

As he rose up, so did her fist. It connected with his jaw, turning it sharply to his right—for a moment. His own right hand swung sharply at her as he turned back. She was barely able to get her left arm up to block it.

From mid-forearm to her fingertips, everything went numb. Everything above that screamed in pain. There was a chance that he broke her arm, and as he pulled his hand back she saw why. The blackjack came at her again, and she jumped back. A tickle went through her hair as the dangerous weapon passed through.

Pussy's eyes darted left and right as she backpedaled. The hall was mostly barren, but not completely. Her right hand wrapped around the column of the torchiere and pulled it up. She wasn't as successful when she tried to grip the other side of the shaft with her left hand. A weak grip slipped off it immediately and it almost fell from her completely. Even so, the base of the lamp clattered along the floor.

The man rushed towards her. Without thinking she thrust the base of the lamp towards his feet. She let go as his legs tangled with the lamp and fell to the ground. The hallway went dark, pulled past the length of the cord plugging the improvised lamp-weapon into the wall. The torchiere and the man spilled down the hall, making Pussy leap up to avoid joining them. Her landing wasn't clean, but it was good enough to let her angle herself so that she fell towards him, landing on his back. Her good hand grabbed a fistful of hair and drove his face into the floor, first once, and then again. The two sharp thumps of skull on hardwood were followed by a more dull sound. She saw the blackjack fall out of his hand and onto the floor.

Grabbing it as quickly as possible, she raised her hand up, intent on bringing it down on the back of his head. He had other ideas. She lurched sideways as he pushed upwards, falling to the left and landing awkwardly on her numb arm. Her face twisted into a grimace as she hit the wall, settling in a sitting position. The man turned to look directly at her, and she back at him.

It became a race. They both went to stand, hoping to get the better angle. The first problem that Pussy saw was that she was starting from a sitting position, while he was already on his knees moving upward. It was a race she was going to lose.

So she changed the game.

Rolling onto her back, Pussy drove her shoe into the man's groin. Her three-inch heels had the desired effect, as he cried out and doubled over instantly. With a wide arcing sweep, the blackjack struck the side of his head, and he collapsed on top of her like a sack of wet paper.

For a moment she simply lay there panting. Catching her breath was tough with an extra one-eighty on her chest, so she pushed and twisted until she was free once more. As she stood, she rubbed her left forearm, trying to push more feeling into it than a river of pins and needles.

"This…sure is easier…when I'm on Fizz," she breathed heavily. She almost regretted leaving it in the clutch that Mr. Crocker was holding for her.

From where she stood in the hallway to the front door were two unconscious men. If there were any more, they surely heard at least that second fight, which meant that they were either coming for her right now, or waiting for her to come to them. She decided to give them that second option. Slipping the blackjack into a pocket, she made her way to the steps.

There was light at the top of the stairs, contrasting the darkness in which she stood. Holding her left arm against her body, she walked up the stairs. Each stair made her crane her head further, looking for anyone who might be waiting. A long railing surrounded the stairwell on the second floor, giving her clear view to anyone walking upstairs, but from what she could see, there was no one.

She let out the breath she had been holding.

Four doors. Hopefully, one of them leading directly to her goal. There was only one way to find out.

The first door opened up to a bedroom with a dirty cot and an even filthier smell. A pile of clothes were in one corner, and a stack of garbage decorated another. She happily closed the door and moved to the second choice.

This one contained a couple dozen cardboard boxes. One of them was open, and it looked like a stack of papers filled it almost to the top. Curiosity called to her, but duty pushed her on, so she closed the door and pushed along.

The next door was locked. She tried to force the knob, but the lock looked new, and wasn't easily coerced. She glanced over her shoulder at the stairwell, and realized that one of the men downstairs—likely the big one—must have the key on him.

With a bit more speed than her ascent, Pussy went down the stairs and to the still sleeping form of the larger man. She rummaged through her pockets, finding many things she would much rather forget, along with a solitary door key. She went back to the stairs and hurried up them.

Just not quite fast enough.

The front door opened below her, and she turned around to see a familiar face.

"Pussy Katnip?" There was a hint of shock in Mugsy's voice, but also a bit of a snarl. "Boss Foxy said you'd be comin' here." He stepped over the unconscious man and began racing up the stairs. Pussy reciprocated by hurrying around the railing and turning to wait. It felt like she barely had time to breathe before Mugsy was on the second story there with her.

"Now, Mugsy," Pussy spoke in tone he should recognize, "there's no need to do this. We both know how this is going to turn out."

"Yeah, that's what I told Boss Foxy." He rolled his neck, releasing a loud series of cracking sounds. "She also told me that wasn't gonna be true this time, and to try anyhow. So...."

He lunged at her. She punched at him. A blow that, under different circumstances, would stop Mugsy cold, simply glanced off his ribs. The impact drove them both down to the ground. Pussy found herself coiling up as a series of blows rained down. Her arms covered her face, but her body was exposed, and Mugsy got in a half dozen solid punches before she threw her elbow up, catching him in the jaw. It wasn't much, but it was enough to move him.

Using that moment of leverage, she twisted and pushed with all her might, and it was just enough to send Mugsy to the floor. She rolled forward, and let her momentum carry herself to her feet. By the time she turned around, Mugsy was already standing up.

She never really noticed just how big he actually was before now. He towered over her, and despite her best shots so far, he didn't look fazed in the least. On the other hand, she was finding it very hard to take a deep breath.

"Let's stop this before it gets carried away." She did her best to not wheeze. "I don't want to hurt you."

"Yeah, I'm not so sure that you can," he answered. "I think Boss Foxy is right, and you just ain't yourself right now, Katnip."

"You're starting to make me mad, Mugsy. You've never seen me mad." Her hand went to her pocket, looking for the blackjack.

"Okay." He smiled. A predatory smile, revealing his wolfish heritage. "I can handle mad."

He moved again, quickly closing the space between them. She waited until the last moment, and then swung the blackjack around, aiming to impact the side of his head. It was a half successful attack. She impacted, but it was his arm. He let out a short yelp, and then in a flash grabbed ahold of the attacking arm with one hand, while the other hand grabbed the blackjack and tore it free.

"A blackjack? Katnip, you don't never use no weapons, so now I know something ain't right." A snarl grew inside his throat as he tossed the blackjack over the railing. "Tables have turned, kitty."

His hands moved, closing around her neck completely. A moment later she felt her feet leave the ground, and then the world twisted and she went straight down. The impact drove her head into the floor and the air from her lungs. And worse, Mugsy came down on top of her. His hands tightened around her throat, cutting off her airway and leaving her lungs empty.

"I ain't supposed to kill you, Katnip," Mugsy growled, "but I gotta tell you, right now feels really good after all those times I was the one on the ground. Feels really good."

Her balled fists struck against him wildly, hitting anything they could manage to find, but she felt her strength fleeing quickly, and Mugsy wasn't moving. She looked into his eyes as tears flowed freely from hers. There was something there she had never seen before. A thirst. A desire for something primal.

And then he yelped and sat straight up. Both of his hands went to the back of his head, and Pussy took that moment to suck in a lungful of air. Mugsy staggered as he stood up off of her, leaning slightly towards the railing. Pussy sat up and grabbed his leg and pushed him up and sideways.

He toppled over the rail. She heard his body crash, tumble, and then crash again. Somewhere in there she thought she heard the sound of a something—likely a bone—snapping.

She turned her head and saw Todd Crocker standing there timidly, holding a blackjack in his hands.

"Are...are you okay?" His voice trembled as he spoke.

"Thanks to you," she managed to force out.

"I just…I saw that man coming inside, and I just couldn't stay out there. I thought I might help," he explained in a weak tone.

"Mr. Crocker, don't apologize. I've never been so happy that anyone ignored what I've said in my life." Her hand went to the top of the railing with the intent of helping her stand. Mr. Crocker went to the other side to make sure she did.

"You don't look so good," he commented.

"I've been better," she admitted. Gently pulling her arm free from his hold, Pussy straightened up under her own strength. "We've got to move. They won't be out too long."

In the course of the struggle, she dropped the key, but it only took a minute to find it on the floor. It fit into the locked door and turned with a click.

Behind the door was a young girl, maybe nine years old, huddled in the corner with her knees up to her chest. Pussy could see her eyes peeking out at her.

"Hi," her voice went soft, though still raspy at the moment, "my name's Pussy. I'm a friend of Jenny's. Would you be Jill?"

The girl's head rose up slightly. Her eyes shifted from terrified to surprised. She nodded slightly.

"Good. I'm glad to meet you finally." Pussy took a tentative step into the room towards her. "Would you like to leave here with me?"

Jill practically leapt to her feet. "Yes. Yes, please. Please can we go?"

"You bet we will." Pussy held out her hand. "We need to go right now, okay."

"Okay." Jill took her hand. The child's grip was strengthened by her fear.

"Let's go." Pussy looked at Mr. Crocker outside the room, and gave him a cue to head out. She picked up Jill, cradling her against her body. Jill wrapped her arms around Pussy's neck, causing Pussy to wince. It didn't slow her down.

It wasn't an easy walk. Pussy walked with more than a slightly noticeable limp, and she had to take the stairs one at a time, and slowly at that. When she reached the bottom, she saw Mugsy. He was lying still, but his chest was rising and falling. His leg, however, was resting at a very unnatural angle.

She stepped over him and walked to the front door.

Mr. Crocker had gone ahead and gotten the car, pulling it up directly in front of the brownstone as she made her way down the outside stairs. When she got to the bottom he had already walked around and opened the car door.

Pussy set Jill down onto the seat, and then slid in beside her. The young girl stayed glued to her side, holding on to Pussy's arm as she closed the car door.

"Where to?" Mr. Crocker asked.

"Your place," Pussy said softly. "And that's where we split up. I'm giving you the job of looking after Jill."

"What?" He looked at her in the rear view mirror. "But…Miss Katnip, look at you. You can barely walk. You need me to—"

"I need you to look after this young girl," Pussy interrupted. "If she isn't kept safe, then I can't do what I need to do next."

"And what are you going to do next?" he asked.

She took a deep breath. Needles stabbed her in the chest as her lungs filled. "I'm going to take the last tooth out of the fox's mouth."

Brett Brooks

Chapter Nineteen

She locked the front door and started walking back down the hallway. There was a surprising lightness to her step that went along with the tune she hummed.

"Well, somebody is in a good mood," Robby laughed. "What's got you actin' all slack happy?"

"It's been a good night," Foxy answered. "Not the night I was expecting or hoping for, but in its own way it's been…almost perfect."

"Really?" He tossed the towel in his hand over his shoulder. "Gimme the news, Sister. What happened?"

Foxy brought her right hand up and casually tossed the hair away from her face, which immediately fell back into place. "Just had a great conversation with some people. Cleared up some things. Set a path for the future."

"Oh, business stuff?" he asked.

"Of a sort, yeah." She brushed past him and walked behind the bar. "How was your night?"

"Like a day at the circus. Fun all the time and clowns were everywhere." He moved behind the counter with her. "A little annoyed at Robin, though."

"What did she do?" An eyebrow raised slightly as Foxy turned her head towards him.

"Never showed up tonight." The towel was ripped from his shoulder and he slapped it against the counter. "She can be a little flighty, but not normally this bad. Whoever she's clobbered for, I hope it's worth it. She was talking him up the other day."

"Really?" With a flick of her tail, Foxy turned around and leaned against the bar. "What was she saying?"

"Wouldn't give me any details, but it was clear that she was totally loco for the guy. Kept going on about it feeling special and all that jazz." The smirk on his face was almost obnoxious. "She was actin' like a schoolgirl fightin' a crush."

"Sounds like a special person, at least," Foxy purred. She stared at the floor, waving her hand back and forth to an unheard tune.

"Maybe. Then again, it's likely just some new ship passing in the night." He shook his head. "Girl gets tied up in these things too often."

Her hand stopped swaying. "What do you mean?"

"Hey, I love my kid sister, but sometimes…. I mean, last year it was that swabbie. The year before that it was some baseball player." He chuckled. "Kid goes through more phases than the moon."

Stepping away from the bar, Foxy moved over to the long row of bottles, moving along them in an inspection without truly seeing any of them. "Maybe this one is different."

"Like I said, I don't wanna talk bad, but I doubt it. She's still trying to figure out who she is. I doubt that some guy is gonna—"

"Maybe this PERSON," Foxy stepped face-to-face with him, "is different. Maybe Robin can relate to them like no one else has been able to before. Maybe it's not just some other man who is there to take advantage of her and abuse her. Have you thought of that?"

"Hey, hey, calm down, Doll." Robby backed away slowly. "You're actin' like it was personal. Do you know the guy she's seeing?"

"What if I do?" The dim light of the club left only part of Foxy's face visible.

The phone rang, cutting off the conversation. With first two steps backwards, and then turning to walk forwards, Robby went to answer it.

Foxy turned back to the bottles. This time she looked at each label closely. A selection of swill with only one or two exceptions. She chose the finest of them, a particularly pricey bottle of scotch in the club for show as much as anything. It rested in her grip, until she let it slip away. It crashed onto the floor like a glass bomb.

"Hey," Robby stood there, blank faced, staring at her, "they, uh, they want to talk to you."

He held the receiver out as she walked towards him. Like a snake strike, she snatched it from his hand and pointed behind her. "Clean that up."

She kept walking until she stood directly by the phone, keeping her back to Robby and the task she had assigned him. Before the receiver hit her ear, she was speaking. "What is it?"

When she picked up the phone her eyes were narrow, and her lips were thin. A few seconds later her eyes were slits and her fangs were bared. She slammed the receiver down onto the phone. The body of the phone couldn't handle the abuse, and broke in half. A few shards of debris fell onto the floor beside her.

"Uh, is everything okay?" Robby asked softly.

She spun towards him, her lips pulled back and open, revealing a full set of canine teeth. "Does it look okay?" In a single motion, Foxy ripped the phone free of its cord and threw it across the club, just over Robby's head. He ducked, and the phone clattered with a faint ringing sound unseen at some place on the other side of the room.

"Jeepers!" He poked his head up above the bar. "What the heck was that about?"

"Idiots. It was about me surrounding myself with idiots. All they had to do was keep one little girl, and…." Long strides took her into the club, before she turned around to stalk back up to the bar. "I was in a good mood. Things were good. Then…then…."

Her fist slammed down onto the bar top, cracking the thick wood.

"Hey, hey." Robby stood up and reached across, moving to touch her arm. She yanked it away before he made contact. "What happened? Is everything okay? You can talk to me."

She laughed. "You really believe that, don't you?"

Robby's eyes were fixated on the crack in the bar. "How did you…?"

"You know, you're right." Foxy's voice turned softer. "I should tell you what's going on. Get your feedback on everything. Finally get everyone involved."

"Involved? Involved with what?" Foxy was already moving around the bar as he spoke, swaying with every step as she approached.

"It's better to just show you," she sighed. Her finger came out and traced along his jaw. "Would you mind…coming upstairs with me?"

"Uh," she saw him swallow visibly, "you, uh, you're actin' a little kooky there, Boss. I'm not sure that—"

"Come upstairs!" She moved her body against his, pressing into him. "I want you, no, I need you to come upstairs with me."

"Hey, Doll, you know I think you're a dish, but," she felt him moving away from her, "maybe another time."

She grabbed his arm. "No. No other time. We're going upstairs, now."

He jerked his arm back. She let it go. "Look, Foxy, any other time and I would be running up there ahead of you, but I'm worried that you're not in a good mental place, y'know?"

"That's why I want you—why I need you—to come upstairs. I need you, Robby. I need you to make me feel better. To remind me that…that everything is going to be okay." Her chin dropped down just enough to let the light hit her eyes a little brighter.

She saw the hesitation in his face. The long pause that eventually led to the answer she knew was coming. "Okay. I don't want to see you upset."

"Thank you," she purred. Her hand went out, extended towards Robby and waiting for him to take it this time. Once he did, she turned and sauntered towards and up the stairs, stopping right in front of the door to their destination. She could feel his heart beating through their held hands. "I want you to know how much this means to me. How much I'm going to enjoy this."

He leaned in towards her, inching his face closer to hers, and she let him. The kiss lingered for longer than she wanted, but it was more a matter of waiting than enduring. Once he broke it and pulled away, she opened the door, waiting for him to step inside.

There was a stale odor that wafted past both of them, but she was the only one who seemed to notice. Robby's mind was focused on—or suffered from a severe lack of focus—regarding a single matter.

He was several steps into the room before she locked the door behind them.

"Would you like a drink?" he asked. "I remember that Pussy keeps a great bar up here."

"It is a great bar, and yes, I am going to have a drink," she answered, "but I'll make it myself."

The moment when he rounded the corner was easily measured by the words that came next.

"What the hell?"

He stood stock still as she walked up behind him. Foxy placed the palm of her hand on the small of his back and looked over his shoulder at what lay beyond.

"It's okay," she explained, "George is perfectly safe there. I just had to make sure that he wasn't going to do anything else that he shouldn't."

She was rather proud of the height. Getting the hook at just the right level took a little work, and a bit of effort, but it was worth it. His feet still touched the floor, if barely, while his arms reached straight up, hung by the rope that bound them together. The mass of bruises that was his face turned to look at them, and his mouth made a motion to talk.

"Rrrbb. Rnn Rbby, shhh hsss Rbbn." The sounds were closer to noises than words, but Foxy understood. The question was, did Robby?

"George?" he whispered. "Oh God!" He ran towards him, while she stood back and watched. "What happened? Are you okay?"

She laughed. "Obviously, he's fine. He won't be causing anyone any trouble there."

It was the look in his eyes that Foxy saw most clearly. Two massive orbs struggling to free themselves from his head. She found it rather comical.

"He was telling you to run, by the way," she explained.

"Foxy, what's going on?" He took several steps backwards. After seven, he stumbled over a chair, because he couldn't take his eyes off of her.

"I'm sorry, Robby, but you just said such hateful things. I can't have an employee like that." Foxy walked towards him. He scrambled to get up off the floor. "And since I can't have you going around looking for your sister, well…."

"What about Robin?" He stopped at her mention. "What's going on with Robin?"

"Nothing bad," Foxy explained. She walked past him, heading to the bar. She moved straight to the crystal bottle with the red liquid inside. "She's keeping me company. She loves keeping me company."

"What are you talking about?"

She removed the stopper from the carafe and brought it to her lips, taking a long drink directly from the bottle. The rush that hit her sent a tremor through her body. "I mean that you should never judge something that you don't understand." She turned back towards him. He took two full steps back.

That was when he ran. He was fully around the corner and heading to the locked door before she took her first step. Yet somehow she was at the door well before him.

"It's actually a good thing, Robby. This way you'll get to see her and keep her company. And I'm sure that she'll make it easier for you to accept things in the long run." Foxy stood between him and the exit, waiting for him to react.

She wasn't entirely surprised when he took a swing at her. Looking over at it, the fist seemed to be moving in slow motion. Several thoughts occurred to her. She could step aside and let him hit the door. She could catch the punch and see how much he liked having his hand crushed. She could simply stand there and let his punch land, just to see what it felt like.

The last option was the one that she chose.

His fist impacted her directly in the nose, causing her head to lash back slightly. There was a slight sting to it, she couldn't deny, but it wasn't that bad. And when the second one landed, there was even less pain. By the time the third one hit her she could hardly feel a thing. Still, that seemed like enough.

When her hand hit his chest, Robby flew all the way back into the main room. He skidded across the floor, smashing into furniture, sending it sprawling. He shook himself, trying to stand up, but it looked like he was too disoriented to manage. It only took a few steps for her to be standing above him.

"It's okay, Robby. I'm not going to hurt you." She reached down and picked him up by the throat. "I just need to make sure that you aren't going to do or say anything else that is hurtful." With a subtle move of her arm, he tossed his body to the wall, landing beside where George was hanging.

Foxy turned to the shelves and removed a candlestick. Robby was still struggling to stand when she made her way to him. Just to be safe, she put her foot on his chest and pressed him down to the ground.

Making a stabbing motion high above her head, she drove the candlestick into the wall. It was buried into the concrete, leaving only what she held in her hand exposed. She reached down to Robby, and pulled his belt free from around his waist. Wrapping it carefully around Robby's wrists, she checked the tightness before picking him up and placing the wrists on the candlestick.

Foxy took a few steps back to check on both men. They looked like ornaments decorating her wall. Or prizes. Awards. Things to remind her of her accomplishments.

"Okay, well, now that we've got that taken care of," she said to both of them, "I need to get back downstairs. Someone has to finish cleaning the place for the night, after all."

She walked down the hall, unlocked the door, and stepped back into the main area of the club. There was a lightness to her step that matched the song she was humming.

Brett Brooks

Chapter Twenty

The doorman was big. Bigger than she remembered. In theory, though, he wouldn't be an obstacle. At least not on the way inside.

"Are you sure this is a good idea, Miss Katnip? I've heard some questionable things about this place." His hand kept tugging at the neck of his shirt. He was more nervous than she was.

"Phillip, I promise you that after we get inside you can leave and go back to the hotel. In fact, I insist upon it." Pussy glanced over at him, her neck hitching slightly in pain as she did, marveling at how different he looked in a tux—even a cheap one—than he did in his bellboy outfit.

"I'm not worried about me, ma'am. I'm worried about you." There was something very earnest in his words. One that Pussy had to agree with on some levels.

"Let me worry about me, Phillip. You're going above and beyond. This isn't the responsibility of The Fountain Royale or any of it's staff," Pussy stated.

"After what happened when you stayed with us, well, both Olive and I agree that you deserve this much," Phillip replied.

"I'm very appreciative, but you did nothing wrong. This isn't your problem. I was grateful enough that Olive loaned me this dress." Pussy stopped on the sidewalk and opened her clutch, pulling out her small compact and opening it up. A quick check to make sure that all the bruises were still well covered by the makeup, and back it went. Her fingers felt inside the clutch for the small vial of Fizz, confirming its location. "Besides, I've got some important business that has to be handled inside."

He tugged at the neck of his shirt again. "Okay, I guess. I'll follow your lead."

Wrapping her arm inside Phillip's, Pussy began walking again, right towards the front door of The Butterfly Club. She could only see the one doorman tonight, and wondered where the others from her previous visit might be hiding.

"Good evening," the bullish doorman said politely. "Welcome to The Butterfly Club." She kept her face down, hoping to stay somewhat hidden—and unrecognized, she hoped. "Have you visited us before?"

"Uh, no. No, this is our first time. Big night out for us." Phillip sounded perfectly awkward. She could hug him.

"Well, there is a minimum cover for couples. It's ten bucks to get inside." The doorman was craning his head out, trying to get a better look at her face, so Pussy turned it to Phillip's side.

"Ten bucks!" Phillip almost screamed it. "I…yeah, okay. Ten bucks, I guess." He fished around in his pocket for a wad of bills. He counted out one after another until they formed a small, very wrinkled stack. She heard the doorman repress a chuckle as he handed them over.

"Again, welcome to The Butterfly Club. Hope you two have a great night." He moved to one side, and Pussy gently pushed on

Phillip's back, rushing him inside perhaps a little faster than he planned.

The smell of stale air and cigarette smoke almost slapped them in the face when they entered. Both of them looked across the room. Phillip's eyes never seemed to go beyond the mass of people surrounding the gaming tables in the center of the space, but Pussy moved immediately past them to the twin doors on the far side of the room. Both doors were open, and three men stood outside them as a living barrier against anyone wanting to enter without invitation.

The sound of singing faintly echoed through those doors, past the crowd, and finally reaching Pussy's ears. A familiar voice.

"We need to go down into the room," Pussy explained. "We're a bit too easily seen where we're at."

"Oh, yeah, sure." Phillip tore his eyes away just as Pussy laced her arm through his once more.

In Pussy's mind they likely made for an unusual pair. Phillip didn't look like he belonged, but hopefully he did look like someone desperate to impress his girl. "In just a moment I want you to go over to the bar and buy both of us a drink. Get me a Singapore Sling."

"Yeah, uh, Miss Katnip, I'm not sure that I have enough money to get us anything after that cover charge. I still gotta pay bills, y'know," Phillip explained softly.

"Well, then just get something for yourself, but get something. I don't care if it's water. I just need you to be at the bar for a couple of minutes. When you come back for me, you either won't find me or you won't like what you find. That's your cue to leave." Pussy smiled at every man she passed as they walked beside the tables.

"So, you want me to spend money to leave?" he asked.

"No, I want you to be gone and give me an excuse to be a horrible girl." She looked up at him. He looked confused. Understandably, in her opinion. "Just trust me. Oh, and I promise to not only pay you back for everything you've spent, but give you a sizable tip for all of this." Her finger tapped him on the chest for show. "Oh, and don't go out the front door. Find another way. We don't need the doorman getting suspicious."

"Where are you going to be?" he asked.

"Hopefully, getting myself in trouble." She leaned up and kissed him gently on the cheek. "Now go get yourself a drink, and I'll see you in a few days."

He walked away, and she walked the opposite direction. On the initial stroll through she spotted her target, and she was now on a beeline for him. There wasn't much room beside him at the table, but that only made it easier to brush up against him as she pushed her way in.

"Excuse me," she cooed at him. "I hope you don't mind me standing here."

It took him less than two seconds to move away from her face so that he could stare at her other features. "No. No, that's fine. Happy to have you hear, Miss…?"

"Collins. Kitty Collins." She held out her hand, palm down. He took it in his and brought it to his lips. They felt cold and clammy against her skin. "What's your name?"

"I'm Buck Dadyr." She thought he fit his name. He was probably quite the buck about twenty years ago.

"Dadyr? That's tough to say." She bat her eyes. "Mind if I call you Daddy instead?"

"That…would be fine." There was a bit of a hitch in his voice. Pussy pretended not to notice. Neither that nor him doing his best to subtly remove his wedding ring. "I can't help but notice you don't have a drink. How about we go to the bar?"

"The baaar?" She let the middle vowel draw out a little long. "That's no fun. I was hoping to have fun." She looked over towards her ultimate destination. "Like there. That's gotta be fun. It's a special place."

"That's a private area. Not open to…." It was probably the quiver in her lip that stopped him, but she added the eyes and the tilt of the head just to be sure. His tone changed almost instantly. "Let's see what we can do."

She giggled, and made a show of it. He extended his arm, and she took it, letting him lead her to the doors—and hopefully what waited beyond. As they got to the door, she angled herself behind him. It was important to choose someone large enough to hide behind, or at least hide enough to not be recognized.

"Evening, lads. Is Mr. Blaid in tonight?" The other thing she needed was someone who looked like he had connections, and appeared tired enough to need a little adventure of his own.

"Mr. Dadyr." They acknowledged him by name. "He is. Were you wanting to join him this evening?"

"If possible, yes." He answered with the confidence she expected.

"Of course. You know the entry fee. Would you like us to put it on your tab?" She recognized the guard's voice. He was the polite one she met the first time here. She turned her face towards her escort's chest.

Whatever the cost of entering, it was enough to make him hesitate.

"Please, Daddy?" The voice sounded far younger than Pussy appeared.

"That's fine," he said to the the kind doorman. "Just put it on my tab."

The doormen stepped aside and the two of them entered.

Pussy wasn't exactly sure what to expect on the other side of the doors. What she found seemed like a scene from an Arabian Nights story.

There were no tables in the room. Carefully arranged in several spots throughout the space were stacks and piles of pillows. Each of these pillowed oasis were populated primarily with men, but there were a fair share of women as well. That is, women who were guests. There were plenty of women at each location, presumably working for the club—and this Mr. Blaid.

Beyond these sultry oasis there were dozens of other women wandering around with trays and drinks. In the corners of the room were dark shadows filled with motion and sound, and that was all the details that Pussy wanted from those. Just outside of the shadows were more of the large, bullish gentlemen that the club seemed to enjoy employing. Without doing a direct count, she estimated at least a dozen.

And then there was the stage. A small thing, barely large enough to hold a single person, but that's all it needed to hold. Jenny stood on stage, holding on to a microphone stand and belting out a ballad that would make a laughing man cry.

"What do you think?" Mr. Dadyr asked, with more than a hint of nervousness.

"It's more than I expected," Pussy answered.

"Not too much, I hope." She felt his hand move over on top of hers. Very gently, she removed it.

"I certainly hope not." Pussy looked at him. "Mr. Dadyr, you should go home to your wife. My guess is that she is probably just as bored as you, and likely to be willing to be very adventurous given the chance. You don't need to be here."

"I, uh, you…." Mr. Dadyr stammered slowly. "What did you say your name was?"

"Pussy Katnip."

She turned at the sound of someone behind her speaking her name. Four men stood there. Two of them she recognized. One of them she knew by name. From the corner of her eye, she saw Mr. Dadyr run towards the door.

"Hello, Bulldog. I hope that your stay at The Fountain Royale ended better than mine began." She looked to the man beside him. "And am I to assume that you are Mr. Blaid?"

"I must admit, I'm surprised you came back," the man answered. "And yes, I am Lupo Blaid."

"No, you're not. You're not surprised to see me at all. No one who has this many guards is surprised by something like this," she answered. From one to another her eyes positioned as many guards as she could. "I don't suppose you're willing to let me leave here with Jenny peacefully, are you?"

"Jenny was a gift from a very special person. I don't relish the idea of her leaving, so…no. She stays," he answered.

"Well, Jenny is an old friend of mine, so I think that trumps being a…gift." Pussy glanced to Jenny, who was staring slack jawed back at her. Pussy quickly estimated the distance between them, and then the distance to both the door and the guards. It was a short sprint for Pussy to the stage. And then the guards were a short punch away from that.

"Oh, but I'm a sentimental sort." He smiled a wolfish smile. A glint of gold shined off his front fangs. "Still, I suppose there is one option. You could replace her."

"Why do I have a feeling it wouldn't be that simple?" Pussy inched two steps to her left.

"Hey, I think having Pussy Katnip working here would be quite a feather. Plus, there are plenty of people who would love to spend some time here with you." His long tongue came out and slid from one corner of his mouth to the other.

"I'm impressed," Pussy said, "you've managed to disgust me in record time." She slipped her hand into her clutch as casually as she could manage. "So, I guess this isn't going to end well, then?"

"Not for you it won't." He nodded towards her. It was all the signal she needed. As her hand moved from clutch to her mouth, she removed the top of the vial with her thumb. The entire contents went down her throat in a single swallow.

The world around her exploded in color. She turned to Jenny, only to see her receding away into the distance. The room pushed forward and Jenny backwards, until she was no longer visible. A muffled sound drew her attention off to her right, and she turned to see Robby tied to a large column, a blindfold over his eyes. The image moved, replaced by his sister, Robin, who was lying flat, caught in a gigantic spider's web, her mouth filled with webs, silencing her screams. The image of Robin rose up, disappearing into shadows. Then there was a huddled, tangled shape, crumpled in the corner. Pussy stared at it, trying to untangle the limbs to make a familiar form. It shifted, moving and turning, until a single limb fell out, and a face could be seen underneath. George's face. He raised up his hand, extending a single finger, pointing towards Pussy's left.

She turned to see a window, drapes blowing into the room. Then a flash of red, and the image of a bottle on a ledge.

The colors faded, and Pussy heard a scream. She dropped down just as the fist swung overhead, catching the tops of her ears and hair. Another fist was dropping down in front of her, but rather than move, she took her hand and caught the side of the wrist, redirecting the momentum of the attack, until it struck the first man in the hip. Not hard enough to do any real damage, but enough to stop him for a second.

Letting go of the wrist, Pussy's other hand moved to the ankle of the first attacker. With a grip like iron she held tight as she stood up. The man tumbled down with an ungraceful slap against the floor.

Spinning around, Pussy's fist led the way, driving into the cheek of the second attacker. He stumbled backwards, but didn't fall. She moved towards him, completely unaware of the other man who had come up behind her.

The blow to the back of her head propelled her forward. Her feet caught up with her as quickly as they could, leaving her in a momentary awkward position. In front of her was the man she punched, himself regaining his footing. She used her momentum to carry her forward into him, driving her right fist up and through his jaw, lifting him off the ground and removing him from the rest of the fight.

Pussy leapt up and over him as he fell, running along towards the stage where Jenny stood. She knew that there was at least one man behind her, and she saw two others coming from either side of the stage. Making a choice, she went right. The man came straight at her, and she mirrored him. He was half again her size, but in her mind that only made him a bigger target. She saw his hand arcing wide in a roundhouse punch, and fell to her knees, sliding underneath and past his moving arm. Her hand came up and latched onto his arm, using the momentum to swing herself up.

Her foot went to the small of his back, and she propelled him directly at the closest pursuer. The two men impacted and fell to the ground, while another ran past him, joining the one coming around from the other side of the stage.

This time, she stood her ground.

A quick punch with her right found its target, hitting him square in his midsection. From the other side a fist flew towards her face. Her head did a quick turn and it missed by an inch. She countered with a shot to the second attacker with her left, and at the same moment, the first one connected with a blow to her ribs. Deep, pre-existing bruises were greeted with new ones, and despite the quick healing thanks to the Fizz now running through her system, her body almost gave out. She refused to allow it. All she let out was a nearly inaudible grunt.

Both of her hands went up to grab the second man's head, and then pulled it rapidly down to meet her rising knee. His head snapped back and his body went instantly limp. There was no time to gloat, as she saw the first man's fist once more heading towards her face. There was also no time to dodge it. She turned her head quickly and braced. The punch struck home, but it was a glancing blow. Still, she felt a warm rush of liquid in her mouth.

Her own hand lashed out again, once more connecting solidly with him, this time in his ribs. She felt the bones give under her fist and heard the air flee his lungs. The other hand swung out wide, driving down as the man doubled over, and finishing his trip to unconsciousness.

The two men who impacted were almost on top of her, and there were two others right behind them. By her count, there were four others after them. The odds were working against her.

"Miss Katnip!" Jenny's voice called out to her, and she reacted, turning to look. The microphone stand was in the air, coming her way. She moved towards it, and in mid stride took ahold of the metal rod.

She spun back and drove the stand like a lance into the man's stomach, stopping him cold. Twisting around, Pussy used the force of the spin to propel the blunt rod into the side of his head. His head turned around, forcing his body to follow.

In a single move, Pussy separated the two halves of the microphone stand, and with half in each hand moved towards the fight. Both hands moved as one. The first rod struck the man who had regained his footing from the earlier assault in the side, while the other met a new attacker directly in his face.

The third man was on her quicker than she anticipated, and despite his effort to hit a more vulnerable spot, his fist only found her shoulder. It was enough to turn her towards him, so she thanked him by bringing both steel rods of the mic stand to either side of his head. He fell straight down and out.

She was able to hear the footsteps of two other men rushing up from behind her. That made five in total, and she was surrounded. There was nowhere to run. She simply had to fight.

Blows rained down all around her. Many of them missed, but almost as many hit home. Still, with as many punches she felt hit her, she felt twice as many land from her attacks. It was only a matter of seconds, but in that time the violence of many minutes were unleashed.

The number of attackers decreased. Five to four. To three. To two. Until there was only the one left. At some point she lost the two halves of the mic stand, but she didn't care. Her fist launched out, sending the final combatant down in a heap.

At first all she heard was her own breathing. Her hand pulled across her face, and she saw the deep red stain on the tattered remains of her dress sleeve. Her mind thought through the events, counting up. Ten. She counted up to ten. That left two guards. Then she heard the quiet whimper.

On the stage was Jenny. Beside her were the two uncounted guards. And beside them stood Bulldog and Mr. Blaid.

"I have to say, Miss Katnip," Mr. Blaid spoke in a slightly hushed tone, "you're more impressive than I imagined."

"Let Jenny go," was Pussy's only reply.

"I don't see a benefit in that." He stepped closer to Jenny.

"The benefit is that you'll get to go home tonight instead taking a trip to the hospital." Pussy stared only at Mr. Blaid.

"We'll see." He reached behind Jenny and pulled out something hidden there. A pair of somethings, actually. He handed one to each of the two remaining guards. Baseball bats. "Take her down."

They leapt off the stage. She jumped towards them. Somewhere in the middle they met.

A baseball bat hit Pussy's forearm, and she felt the bones inside it shift. The other bat came up and caught her in the side, just below the ribcage, driving into her body cavity. Her body screamed in pain, but she remained silent. Neither attack slowed her down.

Her fist sank into the first man's stomach—all the way to the wrist. And she kept pushing forward. The man screamed. Or maybe it was her. Pain or anguish can sound very similar. In either case, that man didn't get back up.

The other one swung his baseball bat again, firmly striking Pussy's back and forcing her to the ground. Right next to the other bat. She grabbed it and rolled onto her back.

He was standing above her, bat overhead, ready to drive it into her skull. His bat came down fueled by his size and position. Her's came up powered by anger and supernatural assistance.

His bat broke in half as hers went through it, and hit him on the side of the face. There was a definite movement of the bones in his jaw as they snapped and dislocated, and he was out before he hit the floor.

She waited a moment, and then used the bat to help push up until she was on her feet. With a slightly staggered motion, she turned around. Both Bulldog and Mr. Blaid were slowly stepping backwards away from Jenny.

Jenny rushed off the stage to her.

"Miss Katnip! Are you okay? Let me help you!" Jenny pleaded. Pussy didn't argue.

Pussy felt Jenny's arm slide under hers, propping her up. She stared at the two men cowering away.

"If I hear either of your names again," she began, "or even think that I have, in regards to anyone I've ever known," she held up the bat, pointing it towards them, "I will be back."

She felt herself moving, and realized that Jenny was walking her towards the exit. Just outside the doors leading to this room a rather large crowd had gathered, staring inside at the commotion and subsequent action. All they looked like to her were nameless mannequins, lined up to display the fashion that was already out of date before it went on sale.

Jenny helped her along, passing through those doors and parting the crowd. The only figure Pussy truly noticed was a lone doorman, the kind one, who stood with his back towards her. The rest of the room was silent, perhaps for the first time that anyone here had ever heard. Pussy barely gave them any notice. The only important part was that no one stood in their way.

Until they reached the front door.

The bullish man filled the doorway, staring inside as they walked towards him. Pussy held out her hand, stopping Jenny, and then stood as tall as she ever had, and looked him square in the eye.

"Try me," she snarled.

Two seconds later he stepped out of the doorway, leaving a clear exit.

The night air felt very cold on her skin, but at least she was feeling something. The Fizz was already fixing some of what was broken. In time it would all be better.

If only she had the time to spare.

"What now, Miss Katnip? Where are we going?" Jenny asked.

She took a deep breath, ignoring the pain. "You're going to a friend's house. I want you safe," she explained. "After that? Well, it's time that I went fox hunting."

Red is the Darkest Color

Brett Brooks

Chapter Twenty-One

She sat in the middle of it all. No chair or stool, she simply sat on the floor, surrounded by the clutter and mess of her own making. Nothing remained on any shelf in the kitchen. One after another she had taken them apart, searching for something, anything, that might direct her towards her ultimate goal.

There was nothing.

No book. No notes. No cauldron or pot that seemed out of place. As the day had gone on she moved past the obvious, and began to tear at the walls and fixtures of the room. The ovens and stoves were dismantled, and the walls were torn down to practically nothing more than studs and braces. The room looked like the storm of the century had torn through, leaving nothing but chaos in its wake.

And in that chaos she found nothing. Her search was done. So, she simply sat down on the floor, surrounded by disaster.

Yet, Foxy was still smiling.

The sound of the door opening and closing was clear to her, as was the rather loud footsteps walking through the room outside. Practically stomping to her ears.

Her mouth popped open and then snapped shut. And then she did it again. And again. Each time, the click of tooth on tooth accompanied her action. Then, just as suddenly as she began, she stopped, stood, and walked calmly towards the door.

At first she only opened it enough to see beyond. To watch as he walked through the room. She was rather surprised when he strode up to one of the premium tables and sat down. Far too casually for her tastes.

The doors banged open like the first fireworks on New Years, announcing her arrival. "Mr. Dogg." Long strides carried her to him quickly. "What brings you here tonight?"

He only glanced her way. "I just came from the hospital. Mugsy's surgery went well. They had to put a piece of metal or a screw or something in him, but they say he'll fine eventually. It'll take him a few months to heal, though."

"Oh, did he have a broken bone?" she asked casually. "I didn't know. Good to hear he's doing well."

"He's not doing well," Dogg corrected. "He's miserable, and feels guilty as hell that the little girl got away." He pulled out the stub end of a stogie and lit it. "Personally, I'm thrilled it happened."

"I beg your pardon?" Foxy raised up and stepped towards him. "What did you just say, Mr. Dogg?"

"I said I'm glad the girl escaped." She watched him put his hand on the lapel of his jacket, and it seemed to her that he poked his chest out a little more as he spoke. "Never should have brought a child into this mess." He looked her directly in the eye. "Oh, and that's Boss Dogg, by the way."

She felt her lip curl up off her teeth. "Interesting," Foxy growled, "I didn't know you enjoyed pain. I can only assume that's true, since you know I'm going to beat you half to death for saying that."

"Why? Because you still think you're boss?" he replied instantly. "Boss of what? Where are the people working for you? Hell, Foxy, you didn't even open the club up tonight. Are you even aware of that?"

"What?" She looked around. The club was empty, and it was late enough that people should be in it spending money. "Well, time got away from me tonight. Besides, it doesn't matter. I don't need them. Or you. Or anyone. I'm the one in control." She covered the remaining distance until she stood over him. "I can do anything I want."

"Really?" Boss Dogg asked. "Then why don't you call your friends?"

It was a casual backhand, but it was still enough to send him flying across the table. "I have friends! Here! In this building with us. They are upstairs, waiting anxiously for me to come see them. They live for my visits."

He struggled for a moment, but eventually Boss Dogg once more stood and faced her. "That sounds more like raving than a statement." She saw a stain of blood coloring the corner of his mouth.

"Are...are you trying to get yourself beaten? Honestly, that's all I can think." Foxy skirted the edge of laughter as she spoke. "I can't see any other reason why you came here."

"I came here because you abandoned Mugsy!" he shouted, ending her laugh. "You abandoned everyone. Everything!" He pulled out a new cigar and held it in his hand. "What happened to you, Foxy? When you first came to us you were filled with ideas and plans. Now you just sit in an empty room and…and I don't even know what."

"What happened? Everything happened!" She spun around, holding her arms wide. "I found a home, and all the things that come with it." Her foot slammed down to the floor with a sound like thunder. "I have everything now, and I won't let anyone take it away."

Boss Dogg's face went pale as she approached. She considered reassuring him that she wasn't going to hurt him—at least not permanently—but chose to let things play out instead.

"What are you doing?" he asked, backing away.

"I'm going to show you just how far I've progressed," Foxy answered. "My plans are…are almost finished. Soon I won't have to plan anything at all. I'll just live the life that I was always meant to have."

"What? What life? You're just playing at being Pussy Katnip right now," he stated. She stopped moving.

"Don't ever say that," Foxy growled. "Pussy Katnip is nothing. She's nobody. Everything that she had was stolen and worthless, and now that she's gone I'm—"

"She's not gone," he interrupted. "You know that. She's the one who put Mugsy in the hospital. We both know that."

Foxy began to trace circles on her dress with her right index finger. "You say that like there's something you haven't told me. What are you not saying, Mr. Dogg?"

"Boss Dogg," he corrected. "And yeah, there is something I haven't told you." She twisted her head slightly to get a better angle as he slowly puffed his chest out further. "I was the one who sent Pussy to the house."

"You…you what?" She was sure that her ears were playing a horrible trick on her.

"Pussy came to me looking for help. I gave it to her." Boss Dogg leaned back onto the side of a table. Foxy's stared blankly at him.

"Why? Why would you do that?" Her voice wavered and raised at the same time.

"Don't you get it? You had us, Foxy! Me, Mugsy, the whole damn town if you had played your cards right. We'd have eaten outta your hand for years, just because of what you did to Pussy. Nobody had been able to get to her. Not even close. But you," his eyes wandered from her feet to her the tips of her ears, "you were something else." And then he shook his head. "Now, you've…become something else."

She returned the favor, looking him over from his toes to the top of his head. "And so you decided to turn against me? Help Pussy?" Her hands balled into tight fists, causing all of her knuckles to crack. "I…." Silence finished her sentence.

"We could have had it all, Foxy. But I wasn't willing to let you take everything." A match flared up in his fingers, and he puffed on his cigar, lighting it. "And yeah, I know what you can do. I saw what you did to Mugsy, so I know that you can—and probably will—put me in the hospital right next to him. The thing is," he pulled the cigar out and puffed out a cloud of smoke, "I'm not scared of you anymore."

"Oh." Her head turned and she looked up at the ceiling. "You're wrong."

"Wrong? About what?" he replied.

She kept her eyes on the ceiling as she spoke. "Everything, of course. Me. Pussy. You. The hospital. All of it." Her head more fell than moved, changing focus from ceiling to him. "Everything."

"The hospital?" was his only answer.

"Yes. Yes, the hospital. You think that you're going to end up in the hospital. No, you won't." She smiled. "I'm going to keep you here. I think…" she glanced back to the ceiling, "…I think I'm going to hang you right over there."

"Hang…me?" The cigar in his mouth was about to fall out.

"Sure. Don't worry, you won't be dead, you'll just be…hanging. Maybe in a cage, or maybe just by your feet or something." She pointed to a spot on the ceiling, near the outer wall. "Right there. Right where I can watch you from stage."

His hand pulled the cigar out before it had the chance to completely fall out.

"People love to see me on stage. Did you ever see me sing?" A sparkle hit her eye. "Oh! You need to hear me sing." Once again she pointed, but this time to the chair beside Boss Dogg. "Sit down, and I'll sing for you."

He hesitated.

"Sit. Down." Each word carried the weight of it's consequence behind it.

His hands found the chair behind him, and then the rest of his body followed.

Foxy began to hum a tune. She walked up to and beyond Boss Dogg, who did his best to follow her with his head. A quick slap of her hand against the side of his face stopped that and turned his attention back forward. She began to sing, softly.

The dog jumped into the fountain.
The dog jumped into the fountain.
The dog jumped into the fountain,
And just what did he find?

The water was too deep.
The water was too deep.
The water was too deep,
And he began to whine.

The others gathered to watch him.
The others gathered to watch him.
The others gathered to watch him...

She stopped singing and leaned down from behind him, putting her mouth directly beside Boss Dogg's ear. His ear twitched, causing him to turn it slightly away, but not far enough that she couldn't finish with a whisper, "Drown there all alone."

He started to move. She grabbed his shoulders and held him in place. If he was struggling, she didn't notice.

"You should be afraid of me, Mister...oh, I'm sorry, Boss Dogg." She held her voice just at a whisper, but loud enough for him to clearly hear. "Because I'm not following any plan, and all I want right now is to find, well, the one thing that is missing from my life." She laughed. "The formula for my happiness you might say. Because, honestly, I'm running very low on happiness at this point."

"And who's to blame for that?" His voice was far more level than she thought possible.

The chair spun around in place, powered by a quick twist of her hands. Now they were face to face again, with her still standing over Boss Dogg. "Don't assign blame. That shows a…a lack of commitment. We're all in this together. We're one big, happy family."

His eyes trembled, even if his voice didn't. "You've gone insane. Completely nuts."

"No, no, no." A spot on his forehead caught her eye. A small bead of sweat was working it's way down his face. She moved in close enough to lick it off his face. "I've never been more sane. I see everything so clearly."

"What…what is it that you see?" His question was punctuated by a deep swallow.

Images flooded into her mind, beckoned by his question. "I see a beautiful day, with me sharing it with the person who matters most to me, and who thinks the same thing back. We're together, surrounded by our friends, there to wish us luck and happiness in our new life. Still, they don't want us to leave, afraid of never seeing us again. So we stay, and not just them, but the city itself welcomes us back, chanting our names." Her eyes narrowed. "But none of that can happen if I don't find my prize, can it? You don't know where it is, do you?"

"Prize? I…I don't know what you're talking about." He squirmed a little, but he didn't try to move.

"The formula," Foxy told him. "The formula to the Fizz. I need to make more, and I don't have the means. I have to have more. Don't you see that?"

"Fizz? I don't understand. Is that something you lost?" he asked.

She laughed. "No. Not me. My mother. She…well, it was stolen, you see. And I have to get it back. It's time for me to get it back."

"Stolen? Who stole it? And what is it? You're not making sense." He swallowed again. "Are you saying that Pussy Katnip took it? She ain't the kinda dame who would—"

Her hand wrapped around his neck, cutting off his words. "She is the worst kind of thief! The type who smiles while she takes something from you. Her family is nothing but a bunch of monsters, happy to destroy everything they touch."

Without any visible effort, Foxy stood up straight, carrying him with her, until his feet dangled just off the floor. "And you helped her, didn't you? The two of you were working together all along! You betrayed me!"

The grip around his neck tightened and the desperation appeared in his eyes. His body began to flail as he beat against her arm, trying to dislodge her grip. Her fingers were just starting to flinch when it happened.

"Foxy!" She knew that voice. Foxy's head turned to see her standing only a few feet away. She looked battered and bruised, wearing scraps of a dress that may have once been nice but now reflected only trouble and despair, and…and exactly how Foxy always wanted to see her.

"We need to talk," Pussy growled.

Brett Brooks

Chapter Twenty-Two

The Kit Kat Klub was never closed. Not for her. The doors might seem difficult to budge, but that was only because most people couldn't see all of the entrances. So, despite the lack of lights, and the sign on the door saying otherwise, Pussy Katnip knew it was open.

There were enough shadows on the streets and beside the club that she was able to make it to the doorway unseen, Pussy was certain. Right now, all she was hoping was that there were enough things on Foxy's mind that she wouldn't hear her opening the door and coming inside.

Her fingers felt along the wall, looking for the cues, the physical indications that would direct her to the handle. Three raised spots beside two indents. Almost exactly where she started looking, in fact.

She pushed in hard and turned counter-clockwise. The click of the lock was loud. Loud enough to make her wince and suck in air through her teeth. Still, she moved on, sliding it to the side and stepping into the short, narrow hallway.

After she closed the door behind her, she was plunged into darkness. She stood still, giving her eyes time to adjust as best they could. It wasn't going to make much difference, but it was better than just fumbling along like a noisy mole. The black turned to midnight blue, and it was enough. Pussy began to walk through the maze-like corridors of the Kit Kat's access hall.

The clinging sensation of passing through spiderwebs fell across her face more than once, and each time she pulled back, despite her own efforts. Courage or not, it was an unpleasant feeling. Especially when bent over and shuffling forward a foot at a time.

The first exit came up on her left, and she paused at it briefly, considering her path. Take this one and she would be back in the main building, able to move more freely, but she would also be out in the open. Better to take the time to get closer before taking that kind of chance.

She would have to pass two other potential escapes from this tunnel at the very least. It took several minutes. She didn't bother counting the exact number. It was more than she wanted, that's all she knew, but she got to her destination.

The panel in the wall shifted under her grip, letting her move it to the side. She never thought of the air inside the Kit Kat as fresh, but after the tunnel, it smelled like a spring morning to her nose. It was a tight fit which made for a very un-ladylike exit, but it put her where she wanted to go: in the club, next to the stairs leading up to her room.

And immediately she heard their voices. One thing about a nightclub is that they are designed to carry sound through the building, and with only two voices, Pussy easily identified both.

Boss Dogg and Foxy Kitt. One of them she expected. The other, not so much. At the moment, it seemed like Foxy was actually singing, though she couldn't make out the words.

In her mind, this was all but perfect. If the two of them continued to argue, they might be distracted enough for her to sneak upstairs without being seen or heard. When she made her way to the corner, just around from the actual stairs, the singing was gone but Foxy was still speaking. Only now, Pussy could make out what was being said.

Foxy laughed. "No. Not me. My mother. She…well, it was stolen, you see. And I have to get it back. It's time for me to get it back."

"Stolen? Who stole it? And what is it? You're not making sense." Boss Dogg's voice sounded nervous, at best. "Are you saying that Pussy Katnip took it? She ain't the kinda dame who would—"

His sentence cut off suddenly, and then Foxy spoke. "She is the worst kind of thief! The type who smiles while she takes something from you. Her family is nothing but a bunch of monsters, happy to destroy everything they touch."

Pussy took a chance and moved her head around the corner. The two of them were at a table. Foxy was standing. She thought Boss Dogg was standing, too, until she noticed his feet fighting to touch the ground.

Foxy was holding him up by the neck with just one hand.

"And you helped her, didn't you? The two of you were working together all along! You betrayed me!"

She looked to her right. The stairs going up were empty. A clean, easy sprint up to her room and what she was certain waited there. The images from the Fizz vision were still clear in her head. Robin, Robert, and George were all trapped up there. They needed her.

And then there was the Fizz. A bottle of it, waiting for her. All she had to do was run.

The sound of Boss Dogg choking cleared all of that from her mind. She didn't have a choice. Not really.

"Foxy!" she shouted the name as she stepped around the corner. And she kept walking, straight towards the pair, stopping just a few feet short of them. "We need to talk," Pussy growled.

The first time Pussy met Foxy, she thought that the vixen's eyes were pools of serenity, easy to find yourself getting lost inside. Right now, the pools were covered by sheen of something slick and oily. A gloss that reflected back too much light.

"You...you came back," Foxy gasped. "I imagined it, but I never thought...."

Boss Dogg was still flailing about in her grip, but each action was becoming noticeably weaker.

"Put him down, Foxy," Pussy ordered. "This isn't about him."

"Hmm?" Foxy looked up at her hand as though she had completely forgotten what was there. "Oh. Fine." Her arm swung out, and Boss Dogg hurtled through the air, crashing through a table twenty feet away. Pussy flinched as though she was going to follow after him, but it was only a flinch. She wanted to rush over and make sure he was alive, but there was something—or someone—that she had to deal with first.

"Tell me," Foxy began, "did you come back to beg? Tell me you came back to beg." There was an unbridled joy in Foxy's voice that sent a chill down Pussy's spine.

"No. Like I said, I came to talk." Pussy kept her eyes on the other woman, hoping to have time to react to anything that she might do, but the Fizz had long ago left her body, and it was obvious that Foxy was still fresh with it.

"Oh. What a shame. I was so hoping to hear you beg for your life." Before Pussy could blink, Foxy was standing less than an arm's length away. "Maybe I'll just make it so you have to."

"You can't!" Pussy replied quickly. "You still don't have the formula, do you? And you've got to be getting low by this point."

It took a moment for Foxy to reply. "Yes. Yes, that's true." Pussy felt Foxy's hand brush up against her face. "You did a very good job of hiding it from me."

"I'll give it to you," Pussy declared softly, "if you let everyone go. George, Robin, Robert, and even Boss Dogg. You let them go and you'll get the formula." She raised her chin up. "And you get me."

"I already have you," Foxy purred, "and everyone else."

"But not the formula. You'll never get it without me," she answered. They stood inches apart, staring eye-to-eye, but Foxy was staying silent. "Fine," Pussy continued, "you want me to beg? I'll beg."

She took a full step backwards, and then Pussy lowered herself down to first her left knee, and then to both knees. She gazed up at Foxy, her eyes moist. "Please, Foxy. I'll do whatever you want, just please, let my friends go. They're innocent. I'm begging you, please, have mercy towards them."

"I don't need to have mercy towards them, Pussy. They're my friends. I'm taking good care of them," Foxy answered. "But, if it makes you feel better, then, well, let's see what they want to do." The feeling of Foxy's hand pressing in on Pussy's face suddenly took her off guard. "But, and listen carefully, you will give me what I want first, or…or I can't promise anything, now can I?"

"Don't worry, Foxy," Pussy pulled back, but her face was held tight, causing the words to distort, "I know what you want. I'll make sure you get it."

Foxy pulled her hand back. "Is that supposed to be suggestive? You forget who you're talking to, Pussy."

"No. I haven't forgotten anything," she answered. Pussy stood up again, her eyes never leaving Foxy. "You agree, then? You'll let them go if I show you the formula?"

With a wide sweep of her arm, Foxy gestured to the stairs. "After you."

It would have been easy to argue. To insist that they go at the same time, but from the moment she stepped into view, Pussy knew that she was going to have to choose her moments carefully. This wasn't one of them.

Four steps up, however, turned into one of them.

"Why, Foxy?" She slowed down, all but stopping. "Why did you do this? You could have just come to me at the beginning. Talked to me about what happened. Told me the truth. You obviously studied me. You know I would have listened."

"Would you?" Foxy snapped back. "History shows that the Katnip family has a selfish side that they like to keep hidden. Or even betray those they think of as dear friends just so they can have a little extra glory."

She turned. "Is that what you think happened?"

"What? You say it isn't? Let me guess, your mother told you differently." The words came with a little venom. "Well, of course the mother of Pussy Katnip would never lie, but my mother, the mother of the poor, derelict Foxy Kitt is a liar. It all fits in a nice package, doesn't it."

"I never said that!" Pussy shouted.

"You didn't have to!" Foxy shrieked louder.

The silence that followed was more deafening than either of them.

"Start walking, Pussy," Foxy's voice went low and soft again. "Start walking or I will grab you by the tail and drag you up these stairs behind me."

There was still a slight hesitance before Pussy turned back. The rest of the stairs fell underfoot like days passing by.

Pussy opened the door to her room and stepped inside. A dank, musty smell hit her nose. One mixed with a rotting smell. It curled both her nose and stomach. "What is that?" she muttered.

"Hmm? Oh, I suppose I should clean. Or have someone clean." A gasp came after Foxy's words. "That's it! Pussy, you can be my maid. You can clean up after me and my friends every day."

"Smells like someone needs to," Pussy muttered.

Only one step into the main area of her apartment, her heart fell. Tied to the wall, their hands high above them, were both Robby and George. Neither of them were moving, but Pussy saw a slight rise and fall from their chest. They were breathing. They were alive.

"Get them down." Pussy didn't turn. She simply spoke with iron words.

"Why? They're perfectly fine. I told you I wasn't hurting them. They're my friends. Unlike you and yours, I don't hurt my—"

"I said, get them down!" Pussy spun and went nose to nose with Foxy. "It wasn't a request for a speech. You're going to get them down or the only potion you'll be seeing is the one to ease the pain from where I'm about to stick my foot."

"Was that a threat?" Foxy narrowed her eyes. Pussy matched her evenly.

"You're damn right it was." Somewhere in the back of Pussy's head, she was reminding herself that a physical confrontation was a bad idea. She was very glad that she could ignore the back of her head.

"Would you like to try, little kitten?" Foxy moved forward, bumping chests. Pussy tried to stand steady, but she stumbled slightly. "The last time we were in this room together, I believe I beat the living tar out of you, and you were in much better condition then, weren't you?"

"Just do it, Foxy." She couldn't remove all of it, but Pussy tried to lower the fury in her voice. "You promised, and I won't show you the hiding place if you don't."

"Hiding place? Up here? I thought we were just coming to visit friends." Foxy looked around the room. "I don't believe you. I tore this room apart looking for it."

"Maybe, but you didn't know how to look for it. This is my place, remember? There are things I don't want anyone finding." Pussy's eyes moved back to her two friends pinned like butterflies on the wall. "Now, get them down."

"One," Foxy responded. "You get one. After I've got what I want, I'll give you the other one. Which one do you want now?"

Pussy didn't hesitate. "Him." Her finger pointed to the one closest to her.

Foxy looked over her shoulder at the person in question. "Of course. Why am I not surprised." With one hand, Foxy lifted him up and off, and then let go. Like so much discarded clothing, he collapsed in a heap. Pussy resisted running over to him. "I'm really not sure why you care so much for him. He's a man. They're all the same."

With those words, it all fell together in Pussy's mind. Everything made sense to her. "Foxy, who is your father?"

The look Foxy gave her was worse than any slap. "What? Why do you care?"

"Did you know him? Ever?" Pussy pushed on, moving closer to her.

Foxy took a step backwards. "If you know what's good for you...."

"He left you. Both of you. You and your mother." Pussy stopped walking. "I understand. My father wasn't in my life, either."

She never saw her move, but Pussy felt Foxy's hand around her throat in an instant. "You know nothing!" Teeth bared, she snarled every word. "I wish I had no one in my life. No... father. After what your mother did—YOUR MOTHER—my mother's mind and spirit were broken. She had nothing, not even herself." Pussy couldn't breathe, and her hands wrapped around Foxy's wrist. "She was easy prey, and ended up being passed around from man to man, each of them taking what they wanted from her and leaving her worse than they found her. By the time I was five I figured out what was going on. By the time I was eight...."

Foxy flung Pussy to the ground. She gasped, grateful to have air in her lungs once again. "You…you were…." Pussy didn't have the breath to finish the sentence.

"Mother died when I was twelve, but that was okay, because her latest was more than willing to take me in. I'm pretty sure that you met him over in Big City." Foxy turned her back and stormed over to the bar, grabbing the bottle of Fizz and taking a deep drink.

"Blaid," Pussy whispered his name.

"Dear Daddy Blaid." Foxy put the Fizz back, and then grabbed the bottle of whiskey resting beside it. "I was surprised it took him a full year before he put me to work."

"Foxy, I—"

"I was good, too." Pussy was cut off, but didn't try to force her way back in. "The best The Butterfly Club ever had. Of course, I had a ton of practice by then. I knew what they wanted, and how to get what I wanted back in exchange. They thought they were using me, but I just…."

A hitch in her voice. That's what it took to stop Foxy, it turned out. She turned her back to Pussy.

"Foxy," Pussy's voice was soft and honest, "it's not too late. What's happening to you, it's not you. You can't help it. The Fizz—"

"The Fizz!" Foxy spun around, tears flying from her eyes. "You were trying to distract me from the Fizz! Well, that won't work, Pussy. I'll make you tell me, one way or another!" Foxy's left hand went to the neck of the hanging man, and her right heel went to the neck of the man on the floor. "Tell me or I'll crush their throats. Where is the formula?"

"Stop!" Pussy jumped to her feet, her hands open and before her. "I'll get it. Just…just relax. I'll get it." She only took one step before Foxy responded.

"Oh no. No no no no no." She let go with her hand and stepped over in front of Pussy. "I'll get it. You tell me where it is."

There was a moment where Pussy considered her options. The consequences of what she was about to do. A quick glance over at her friends was enough to convince her. "Behind the bar. You have to move my bar, and there is a small room behind it. You'll find what you want in there."

"The bar." Foxy turned back to it. "Why didn't I think of that?"

"Because, you didn't want to," Pussy answered.

"Don't move. Don't do anything." Foxy walked towards the bar. "I won't be long."

Pussy was well aware of that fact. She watched Foxy stand in front of the bar, studying it. And then, using her left hand, Foxy picked up the bottle with a trace of Fizz left in it. Her right hand grabbed the bar and flung it aside. The sound of glass and wood breaking apart filled the corner of the room, and was even loud enough to make both men flinch.

The small opening near the floor was exactly the way Pussy remembered it. Now, the question was whether or not it held Foxy's attention.

Foxy looked back over her shoulder. Pussy looked up at her as she did. "Like I said, don't go anywhere. You won't get away."

"I know," Pussy answered.

And with that, Foxy went into the hole. Immediately, Pussy ran to the window. Her friends would have to wait, just for a few seconds more. If she was going to get them out of this, she needed to find out if the vision she had in The Butterfly Club was accurate. The sash went up, and half her body went out the window.

There was a bottle. A bottle partially filled with a very familiar red liquid.

Bottle in hand, Pussy pulled herself back inside. There was no time for ceremony or thought, she simply pulled the stopper free and drank. And drank. And drank. She'd never taken this much Fizz before, but this was her only chance. It was everyone's only chance.

The bottle slipped from her hand as the Fizz took hold. In the dim recollection of reality, she thought she heard it bounce off a chair and then rattle to the ground. Empty, but unbroken. She definitely felt herself floating. Slipping and falling through air as thick as pudding, wondering if there was a bottom to this odd well. She couldn't be sure, because all she could do was feel. Her ears were filled with a roaring pulse, like the sound of a thousand drums beating inside her. And there was no chance to see anything at all. All she could see was red.

Something hit the back of her head. And then the rest of her body. Almost all at once she felt everything impact against her from behind. Then, just as quickly as it began, the world snapped into place. It took less than a second to adjust, but it felt like minutes to her.

She was on her back, lying on the floor. The empty bottle of Fizz inches away from her.

Springing up off the floor, directly to her feet, Pussy raced over and pulled the other man off the wall, lying him down next to the first. That's when she heard the slurred whisper.

"Izz ntt…ntt pyyrr." It was George. She leaned in closer.

"What? George, lie still. I've got to try to get you both, and Robin when I find her, out of here. Foxy won't be long. Those are just access tunnels, she—"

Even tied, he managed to grab hold of her with his hands. "No." His voice was stronger. "Her...her Fizz. I mixed it. Took half and put it in bottle. Other half mixed with...with...."

He fell unconscious. She didn't dare try to wake him back.

"If that's true," Pussy mused aloud, "that means she was drinking a diluted version of Fizz." She stood up. "We might be on even ground."

"Pussy!" The roar proceeded Foxy by only a second or two. She burst through the hole in the wall, rising up and snarling in anger. "You lied to me!"

"I did," Pussy admitted. "I had to."

"That...that wasn't very nice." Foxy rolled her neck. "I'm going to have to do something...rash. I didn't want to do that, you know, but I need you to get me that formula. So...so I'm going to have to hurt someone."

"There is no formula." Pussy stood between Foxy and the men on the floor.

She could almost see the words rattling around in Foxy's brain. "What did you say?"

"Not like you want, anyway." Something warm ran through Pussy. She could feel the air touching her skin. All of the pain wracking her body disappeared. "The only person in the world who knows how to make it is me. It's never been written down, and never will be. I'm the formula, Foxy. I'm the way that Fizz is made."

"You…you…." Foxy's hands went to the sides of her head, then up to her ears, grabbing and pulling backwards until her fingers slipped off, and the ears snapped back into shape. "YOU!!"

Foxy's leap was impressive. She was easily going to cover the space between Pussy and she, with plenty of momentum to carry them both to the ground in an apparent tackling move. That is, if the whole thing wasn't going so slowly to Pussy right now.

Just as she got close enough, Pussy grabbed hold of Foxy's extended hand, and then spun, adding her own force to Foxy's leap. Like a rag doll, Foxy twisted and turned as she flew through the air, until she impacted the wall on the far side of the room and then slumped to the floor.

Before the sound of her body hitting the floor faded, Foxy rose to a single knee. A smile traced her face from ear to ear. "Oh. Oh, yes. It seems the little kitten still has claws."

"Sharp ones." Pussy ran towards her, and Foxy stood up to meet her squarely.

They met in the middle. Their hands locked and their fingers interlaced. Arms pressed and shoulders bulged out, as each one tried to push the other back.

"This…this is how it should be," Foxy hissed. "I'll prove that I'm better than you."

"It's not…about who's…better." Pussy pushed the words out slowly. "We were…meant…to work…together."

"Work with you? Are you that stupid? You ruined my life!" Foxy howled and rose up higher, angling down.

Pussy felt her knees buckling.

It was only a matter of time. So, Pussy sped things up a bit. As she fell backwards, Pussy made sure to keep a solid grip on Foxy's hands. At least until Pussy was able to wedge her legs up and plant her feet on Foxy's chest.

With the shoving kick, Foxy flew backwards. If it weren't for the furniture that she destroyed in mid-flight, Foxy would have likely hit another wall.

"Okay," Pussy mused as she regained her feet, "maybe not quite a level field just yet." She smiled. "But it is much closer than before."

Foxy stood. Pussy turned and ran. Foxy followed.

The room's closed door barred Pussy's way, but she refused to let it slow her down. Her shoulder burst the latch off the jam, putting her on the landing overlooking the club and the stairs going down to it. She opted not to use the stairs.

The leap over the rail was easy, the landing twenty feet below not as much. She sprang to her feet and kept moving. She wanted to be in the middle of the tables before Foxy caught up to her. Already she heard Foxy land behind her, following her course down. She had already closed half the distance. There were four, maybe five seconds left.

Plenty of time.

Three tables in she hit the top with her hands, catapulting herself up and over it. Foxy's hands hit the table just as Pussy's left, and the table couldn't take the damage twice. It broke in half, shattering the legs and falling away as Pussy landed beyond it. She had another second, maybe two.

"Running? You think that's going to save you?" Foxy screamed.

Save her? No, Pussy knew it wouldn't do that, but she also realized that she needed some sort of edge if she was going to win, and the only one she had was the fact that she knew this club better than anyone.

Table six. The one with the rickety legs. She ran past it, pulling the leg free as she did, and then immediately turned and attacked. The overhand strike was quick and powerful, but Foxy still got her forearm up in time to block it. The wood shattered, sending shards of wood flying. She hoped it hurt Foxy as much as it did the table leg.

If it hurt her, it certainly didn't stop her. Foxy powered her fist into Pussy's midsection, driving the feline's body back and the wind from her lungs. She had no time to recover, either. Foxy's fists seemed to come from every direction. All she was able to do was bring her body in tight and wait for an opening. Blow after blow struck her body, leaving what she was sure would be memorable bruises behind. They did not, however, take her out of the fight.

Foxy pulled back to deliver a haymaker, and Pussy moved in. Short, sharp punches impacted in and up below Foxy's ribs, working her body like a prize fighter. The moment she brought her arms down, Pussy changed angles, sending out quick jabs to the face. Two, three, four times Foxy's chin recoiled as Pussy's fists found their target.

It is entirely possible that five would have been enough to make a difference, but Pussy would never know.

A howl, as much from frustration as pain, signaled Foxy's attack, and Pussy could do nothing to stop it. Any attempt at fighting was gone, as Foxy turned this into an open brawl. She launched herself into Pussy, driving the pair of them into, and through, the remains of table six. Both it and two tables beside it flew like bowling pins in a perfect strike. Chairs went up into the air, crashing down around them as the two women tumbled through the wreckage.

Eventually, Pussy landed on top of Foxy, who raged at her from below.

"Stop this, Foxy! We don't need to fight!" Pussy urged.

Foxy's hands slammed into Pussy's chest, sending her flying backwards, and landing flat on her back. The shadow of Foxy appeared above her, like some great predator of old dropping down on its prey.

For the second time that night, everything slowed down. The descending form was nothing more than a silhouette in the dim light of the club, with white tinged highlights of fangs and claws. In that moment, Foxy appeared to her as a harbinger of death. A creature from the darkness here to take her life. And in that one fleeting instant, Pussy felt fear.

With every ounce of strength she had, Pussy rose and propelled herself up, catching Foxy as she fell, twisting them both around, and then driving into the debris. More wood splintered, showering out and away from the impact. Immediately, Pussy pulled back and stood.

Foxy didn't.

She stared up at Pussy, her eyes burning with hate-fueled fire—and then dimming.

"What…what did you do?" Foxy asked.

Pussy took a step backwards and to the side, trying to gain a better position. Still, Foxy didn't move.

"What did you do?" Foxy shouted.

This wasn't a ploy, or at least Pussy was fairly sure it wasn't. "What are you talking about?" she responded.

"I can't move! I can't move anything!" Her head turned slightly, but no other body part shifted at all.

"Oh no," Pussy gasped. She saw a small red stain appear below Foxy. She immediately dropped down beside her. Her right hand slipped carefully below Foxy's back, a large chunk of wood was there, right at the base of the spine. "Oh, please no."

"What did you do to me?" Foxy screamed at the top of her lungs.

"I…you fell on top of some wood. I think…I think it was the other side of the table leg I broke off. The part that was still on the table. It's…it's driven into your back," Pussy explained.

"Why can't I move?" The volume of Foxy's voice went down, but the insistence behind it remained as intense.

"I…I think that it's in your spine." Pussy whispered.

She said nothing. Foxy stared up at her silently for a full three seconds before her face started to contort. Another three seconds later she broke out in intense laughter.

"Pussy?" The voice was weak, but clear. She turned to see both George and Robby standing—more leaning—against the rail on the balcony overlooking the club. George was speaking. "Pussy, are you okay?"

"Call an ambulance, George! Hurry!" Pussy turned back to Foxy, whose laugh was starting to fade away.

Tears streamed down her face.

"You did it, Pussy," Foxy's voice cracked. "You broke me. You literally broke me. Time and I couldn't tell you how many others have tried over the years, but it took someone like you—a Katnip—to finally break me. I guess it's in your blood."

"Relax, Foxy. We're getting an ambulance. Someone will be here soon," Pussy replied calmly.

Foxy continued without acknowledging her. "Don't you get it? It's tradition. Your family is the destroyer. The one who takes everything away from my family."

"Don't think about it, Foxy. Just…just relax," Pussy said.

"I am relaxed," Foxy answered in a calm voice. "It all makes sense, don't you see? It's a perfect circle. Nature being true to itself. I won. You lost. I'm the victim." Foxy smiled. "And you, Pussy Katnip, you're the monster."

She sat down beside Foxy and held her hand. It didn't respond to her touch at all.

"I know I am, Foxy. I know."

Brett Brooks

Epilogue One

She stepped from the building just as he was walking up the stairs. For a moment, she considered making a joke about coincidence and timing, but that faded quickly.

"Hi, George," Pussy pulled her clutch in to her chest, holding it delicately.

"Wow." George let out a short whistle. "You, uh, you look great."

"Thanks. I wanted to make a good impression," Pussy explained. That was partially true. The hospital really didn't care if she wore her black skirt and black gloves with her white jacket. Not to mention the white suiter hat with the black band. "Did you find out about Boss Dogg?"

"Yeah. He's fine. A little worse for wear, but healing up quickly. He's actually in the same hospital room with Mugsy. I figure they are already plotting your demise. They'll be back to being a thorn in your side soon enough." George was in his formal dress uniform. She took note. "How are things here?"

Pussy glanced back. The Tyler Institute. She was a little too familiar with it. "I don't know. I'd like to think that they'll be able to help Foxy. They helped my mother after her initial breakdown. Got her back on her feet once the…. She developed a situation that is still haunting her, but that was different. Foxy is, well, she's still convinced that I did this to her on purpose. She keeps going on about how my entire family abused her, and then following it up with threats to kill me and everyone else in the building. She's still recovering. I'm hoping she gets better."

"She's lucky to be alive, Pussy." George put his hand on her forearm. She didn't move it.

"That's the Fizz," she explained. "If it wasn't for that, she would have died. Instead, she's…paralyzed. For anyone else, it would be permanent, but I can't say for certain about her. None of the doctor's can. They have no explanation about how she's been able to heal from the surgery so quickly."

"And you didn't explain?" George asked cautiously.

"How could I?" Pussy moved her arm, circling it inside George's and taking a step forward. He took the hint and walked with her down the stairs. "But, honestly, that's not what has me worried. I'm far more concerned that they won't be able to help her mentally. She's so far gone."

"And that's not your fault, either." There was a tone in George's words.

"You think I'm blaming myself?" she asked.

"Aren't you?" He nodded backwards, towards the building she just exited. "You're paying for her treatment, and I know that isn't going to be cheap."

"What am I supposed to do? Leave her out on the street? I can't. Not after…. And I can't take care of her myself, and taking her to Mother's house is out of the question." Pussy's laugh was almost a statement of its own. "Foxy's reaction to me would be calm compared to what she might say to my mother."

"So you're just going to let her drain your bank account?" George tipped his cap back slightly as they stepped off the stairs and onto the sidewalk.

"I'm going to try to make her better. She's just sick, that's all. She had no idea what the Fizz would do to her. Neither of us did, honestly. And she drank so much of it. It could have killed her, given time." Pussy smiled over at him. "Though, if it weren't for you, I don't think either of us would be here right now. I have you to thank for that."

"Me?" His head recoiled to the side.

Pussy pulled herself closer to him. "You were the one who put aside some Fizz for me and then diluted what she had left. We're lucky she didn't notice the difference, actually. I suppose at that point she was totally delusional, though."

"That reminds me," he began, "how did you know about the Fizz out on the ledge?"

"I saw it. In a vision when I drank the last dose of Fizz I had with me. I told you about them. I had one of the bottle you put out there," she explained.

"But not about the diluted Fizz?" He stopped walking and turned to her. She did the same.

"I don't see everything. Just...glimpses. Things that are important. That will become important. I saw Robin, Robert, and...you. And I knew where you were, and then the bottle on the ledge."

"Yeah, okay." The words came out very slowly. "I'm just going to have to take your word on that one. But," he looked back at the institute, "do you really think she's going to get better? And what if she just heals and then comes after you again?"

"She won't. There is a lot of Fizz in her system, but it's fading. Even if it does heal her back, she won't be a threat anymore." Pussy looked back with him.

"You can't know that." He looked back at her. "Unless you had a vision about that, which I doubt. And even then—"

"George." She put a finger to his lips. "Foxy is my responsibility. Don't you worry about her. I'm going to make sure that she stays safe and as harmless as possible."

"I know, but you still can't—"

"George!" She put her hands on either side of his face. "Shut up."

As gently as she could, Pussy pulled his face down towards him, until their lips finally met.

He didn't say a word.

Red is the Darkest Color

Brett Brooks

Epilogue Two

She stood on the balcony, overlooking the club. Below her people scurried about, preparing for the second most important night in the history of the Kit Kat Klub. For the past two weeks, Pussy had kept the club closed, allowing time to properly repair the club—as well as all of its important contents.

Now, everything was back. And more importantly, everybody was back as well. She looked to the stage, and saw the first person she wanted to speak with tonight. Living up to her feline heritage, Pussy sashayed down the stairs, enjoying the sensation. A turn to her right, and a few smiles at the staff, took her to the stage.

"Good evening, Jenny." Her voice was clear and strong, but smooth.

"Miss Katnip!" Jenny almost jumped off the stage, only hitting two of the five steps on the way down. "How are you?"

"Don't worry about me," Pussy answered. "How are you? You ready for this?"

"More than you could imagine. It's like coming home again." Pussy saw Jenny pause and gather herself. "I…I don't think I've really said how much I owe you. How much my sister and I owe you."

"Don't worry about it, Jenny. I'm just glad you made it back to us here. You're right, this is your home. I want you to think of it that way." Pussy pointed to the stage behind Jenny. "I want you to think of that as your home. You deserve to be up there."

"I'm just a placeholder for you, Miss Katnip," Jenny stated.

"Actually, I was wondering if you would do me a favor tonight, seeing as how it's our grand re-opening," Pussy began. "How would you like to sing a duet? I know we haven't practiced anything, but—"

"Yes!" Jenny blurted. "It would be an honor. Thank you."

"No, thank you." Pussy stepped over and hugged Jenny softly. "Now go ahead and finish up your prep. You're our opening act tonight, you know."

Jenny said nothing else. She just smiled and ran back up on stage.

"Miss Katnip?"

Pussy turned around, confirming the surprising voice she heard behind her. "Robin? Robin, what are you doing here? I told you to take time off until you were ready."

"I am ready," she answered. "That is, if it's okay with you." Robin stared up at her from below her eyelids.

"Of course. I said when you were ready, so, if you say you are…." Pussy raised a finger. "But, I want you to promise me that you aren't just doing this out of stubbornness. You being healthy is far more important than this club. Your job isn't going anywhere."

"But I am better, thanks to you," Robin's eyes fluttered. "If you hadn't shown up and saved me—I mean, us, you know, Robby, George, and me—well, I'd just be…. I don't even know."

"Like I've already told you, you're very welcome. I'm just glad that I was able to help. If Foxy hadn't slipped and fallen on that broken table, well, who knows what would have happened?" Pussy half truth was covered by walking towards the bar. Robin fell in right beside her.

"You would have done something. I'm sure of it." Robin said. "You're just…."

"I'm just like everyone else, Robin." She glanced down at her. "Just lucky to be here."

"Oh, no! No, that's not true. You're not like everyone else. You, well, gosh, you're just…." Robin ran ahead of Pussy and turned. "You're amazing."

The impact of the hug was almost enough to knock Pussy backwards. The kiss on the cheek was almost as jarring. Before Pussy could respond, Robin ran away, giggling like a school girl.

With a small sigh, Pussy continued her path to her destination. Stepping behind the bar and walking up to the sink.

"You've left quite an impression, boss."

She didn't even turn. "So it would seem, Robert. How is she doing? Honestly?"

"She's a tough kid, Miss Katnip. Still, I gotta say she's doin' even better than I woulda thought." He moved to stand near her, leaning against the back bar. "She, uh, she's got a, uh…. Robin really thinks the world of you, boss."

The clean bottle came up out of the sink and Pussy shook it a couple of times to get some of the extra water out of it. "So it would seem."

Pussy moved to the corner of the bar and picked up an unlabeled bottle. She took out the stopper and poured a small portion from the full into the empty, and then moved a few feet down and repeated the action with a different bottle, adding to the newly cleaned container.

"Oh, I don't mean it as a bad thing, y'know. She just…." he hesitated. She stepped past him and picked up a pair of bottles, adding a portion of their contents to her new one.

"Don't worry about it, Robert. I'm very fond of Robin, myself," Pussy stated. Three feet down the row she pulled a bottle from the back row and poured a shot into her quickly filling bottle.

Robby hadn't moved, but he was watching her every action. "Y'know, I never have understood you about this."

"About what?" she asked.

"This drink of yours. I've seen you make it a dozen times, and it always seems like you do it a different way," he stated.

"Does it?" She moved on down to the end of the bar. "I hadn't noticed."

"Yeah, I mean, most of those bottles you pour outta aren't even labeled. How do you know what's in them?" he asked.

"I put them there," Pussy answered as she picked up a tiny bottle from the front row of the back bar. She held it up for Robby to see, and then poured a couple of drops into the bottle.

Placing the stopper back in the top, she swirled it first one direction, and then the other. When she set it down on the counter it gradually transformed into a deep red color.

"I can't believe you drink that," he said. "I tried it once, you know. That stuff tastes awful!"

"Well, it's an acquired taste, I admit," Pussy chuckled.

"What is it, anyway?" he asked.

"This?" She picked up the bottle again and stared at it's contents. A dark reflection stared back at her from the glass. "This is nothing but trouble."

"If you say so, Miss Katnip." Robby shook his head slowly.

She sat the bottle back down and turned to look at him.

"Robert...Robby, please," she smiled over at him, "call me Pussy."

THE END

Brett Brooks

Afterword - Why Pussy Katnip?

And here we are.

I certainly hope you enjoyed *Red is the Darkest Color*. As I
mentioned in the foreword, I expand on Pussy's origin quite
a bit, which ultimately formed the basis of the novel. I didn't
want her to have a clean origin, but rather something that
created not only a physical, but also a psychological issue for
her. She has amazing powers, but they come at the cost of
heavy addiction and possibly her own sanity. Not something
you normally think about in an anthropomorphic cat girl.

There was a period where this was NOT a Pussy Katnip
novel, by the way. This is a pulp-noir superhero story first and
foremost, and one that I enjoyed telling, but did it need to be
a Pussy Katnip story? Was there anything in the story that
demanded that the characters be anthropomorphic animals
living in a noir world? No, not really. So, at first this was about
a new character simply inspired by Pussy and her world.

That's when Bobby Politte comes back into the story. I was
telling him about the novel, and even had him read the first
chapter, and he came back to me somewhat disappointed. Not
with the story, but with the fact that it wasn't Pussy Katnip. He
wanted a new Pussy Katnip story, not a pastiche of a character

that virtually no one really knows. To him, the book was going to be a disappointment if it didn't feature her and her rather unique world.

He was right. Pussy isn't someone who should be swept away. This is a story about a girl who has a potion granting her super powers, who is the owner and star at her own nightclub in Mutt Town, the run-down section of a bigger city, with a cast of characters all around her. She's a bit of femme fatale and a bit of pulp crimefighter all rolled into a blond, feline package.

The story was reworked, making it central to Pussy and her cast of characters, and I couldn't be happier.

I truly hope you enjoyed this book. It was definitely a labor of love, in the oddest sort of way. I want there to be more of them, too. The second novel is already in the plotting stage, in fact. Her ultimate fate is in your hands, though. If no one else wants these, then she might fade away once more. I certainly hope not. Pussy deserves better than that.

So, leave a review. Tell a friend. That's the lifeblood of books like this one. Let's keep Pussy Katnip alive for a long time.

Thanks for reading. See you again soon.

- Brett Brooks